MW00944016

The Untimely Passing of Nicholas Fart

A Who-Dealt-It Mystery

written by *Josh Crute* • illustrated by *James Rey Sanchez*

HARPER alley

An Imprint of HarperCollins Publishers

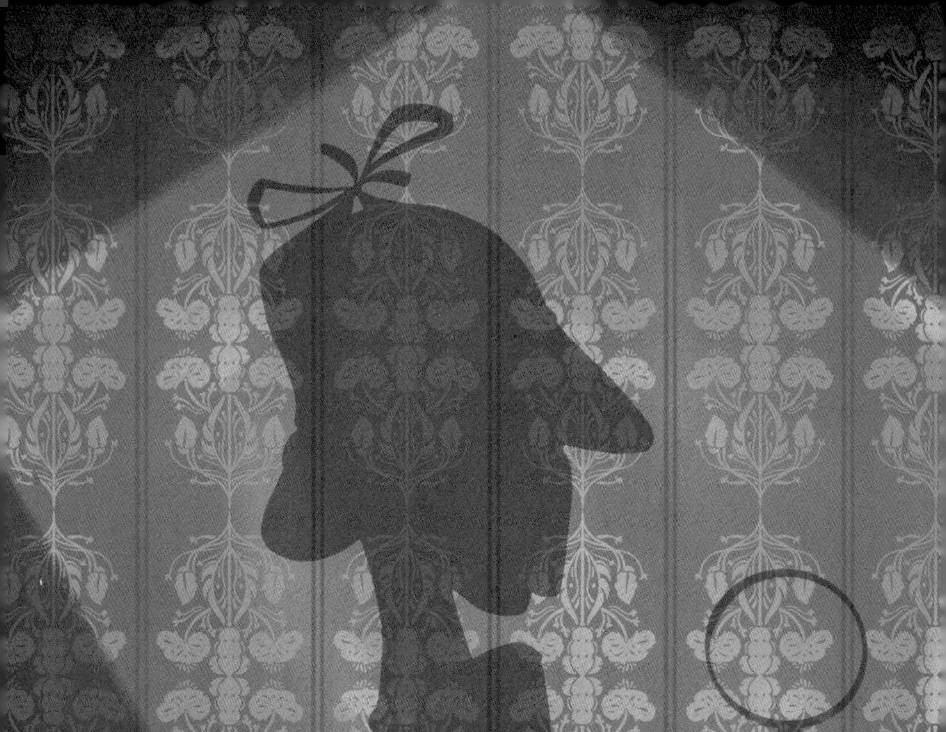

HarperAlley is an imprint of HarperCollins Publishers.

Super-Serious Mysteries #1: The Untimely Passing of Nicholas Fart

For information address HarperCollins Children's Books, a division of HarperCollins Publishers, 195 Broadway, New York, NY 10007.
www.harperalley.com

Library of Congress Control Number: 2022948044
ISBN 978-0-06-309339-3 — ISBN 978-0-06-309338-6 (pbk.)

The artist used Photoshop to create the digital illustrations for this book.
Typography by Joe Merkel
23 24 25 26 27 GPS 10 9 8 7 6 5 4 3 2 1
First Edition

A WARNING FROM DETECTIVE GLUM

So, you want to be a detective, eh? Well, listen. Solving mysteries is serious work. Super serious.

Trust me. When you've been a detective as long as I have, you'll know there's nothing silly about it. Especially when stinky smells, awful odors, passed gas, SBDs,* and other such heinous crimes are involved. The mystery you are about to read contains all of them and more, so proceed with caution.

And whatever you do, don't breathe through your nose.

Sincerely,
Sirius Glum

PS I'm serious.

*Silent-But-Deadlies

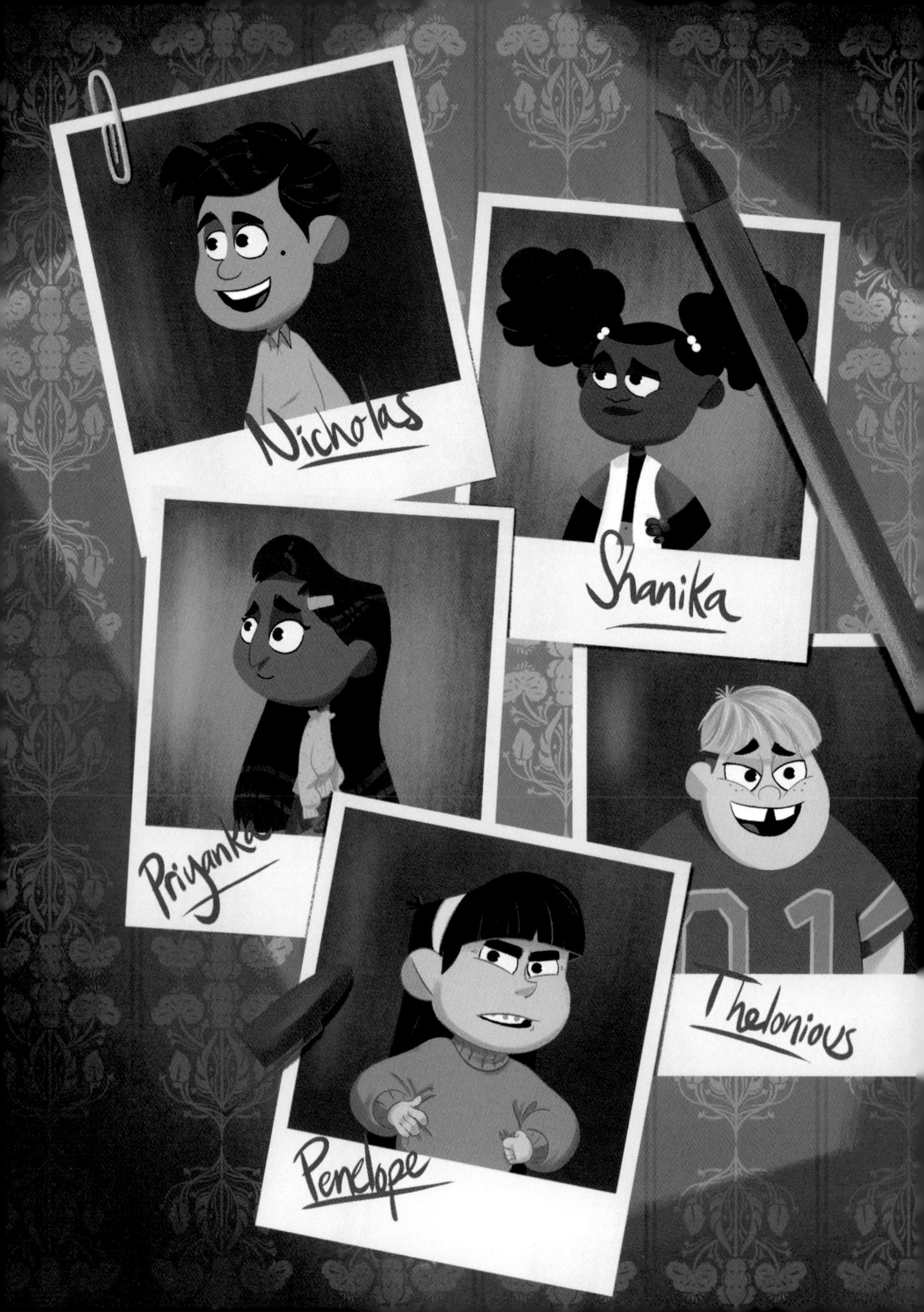

Nicholas
Shanika
Priyanka
Thelonious
Penelope

TABLE OF CONTENTS

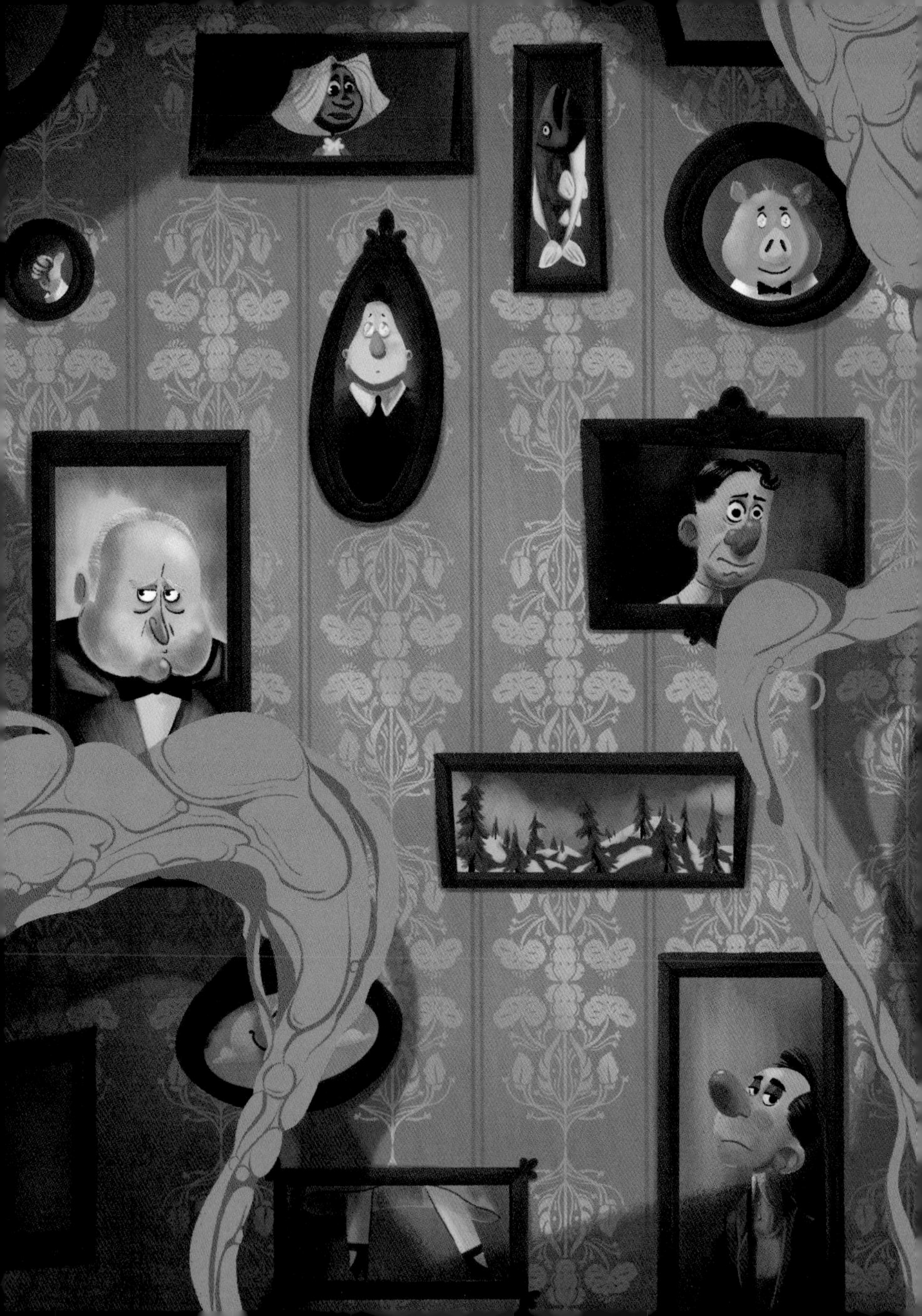

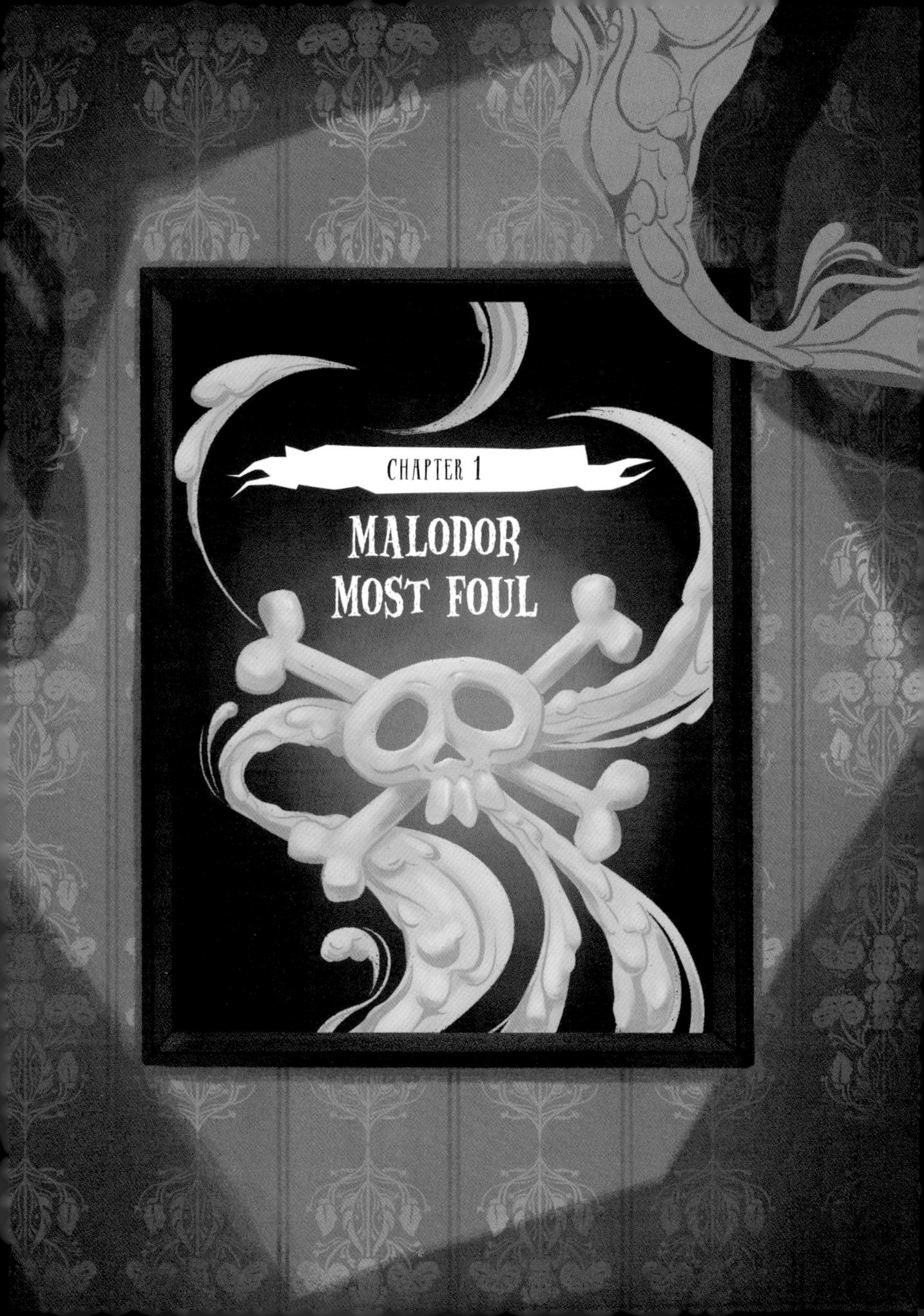

CHAPTER 1

MALODOR MOST FOUL

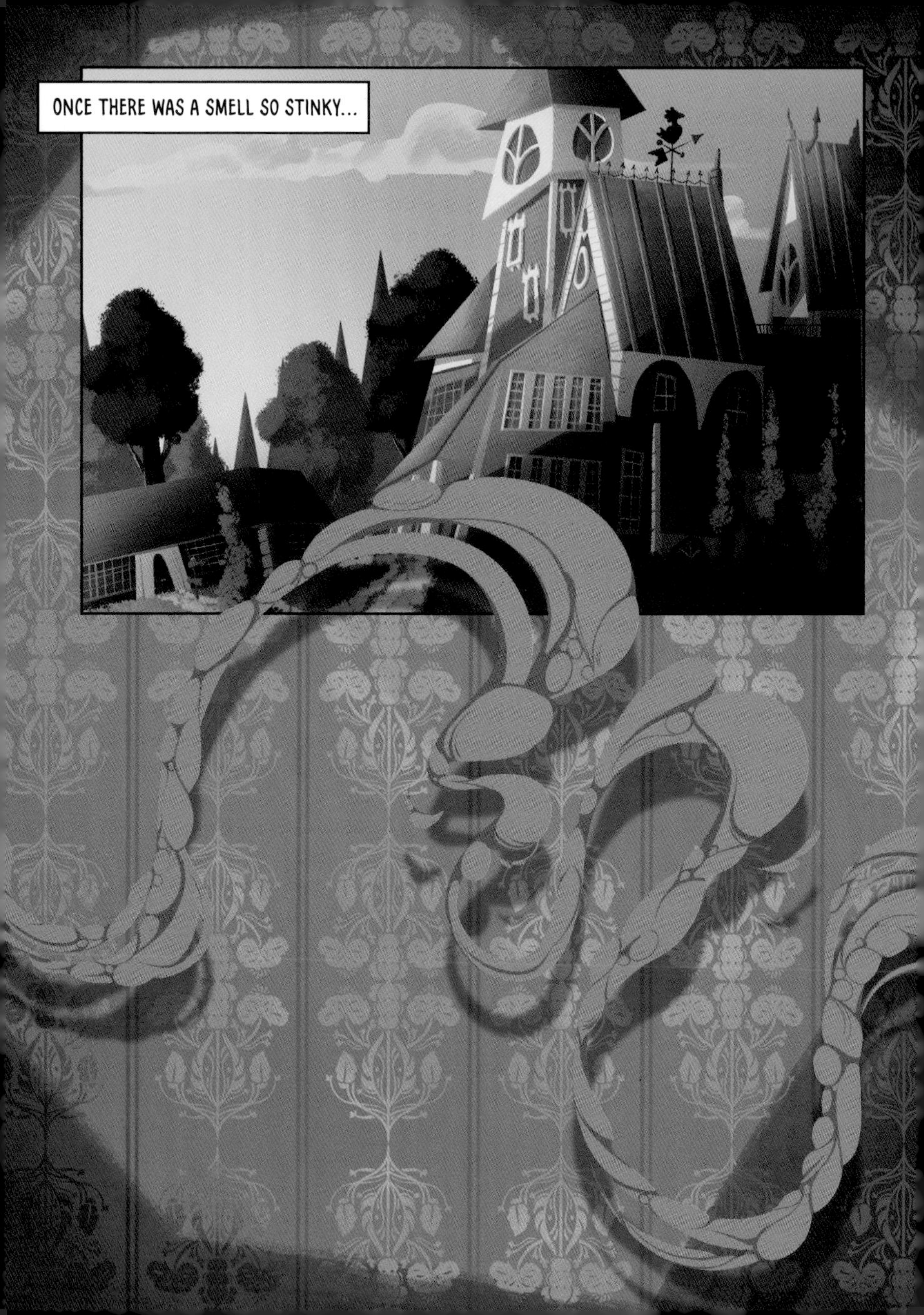
ONCE THERE WAS A SMELL SO STINKY...

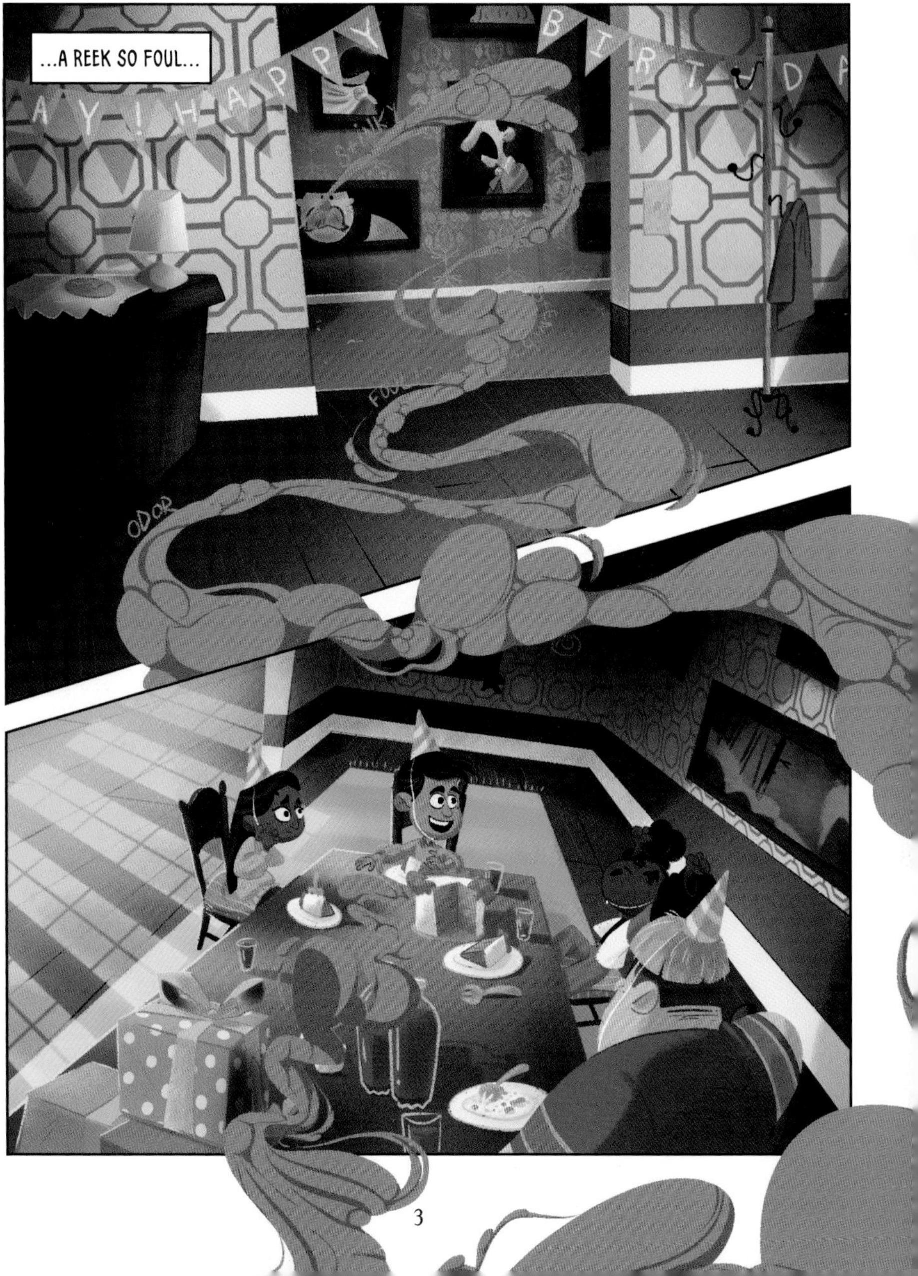
...A REEK SO FOUL...
AY! HAPPY BIRTHDA
FOUL
ODOR

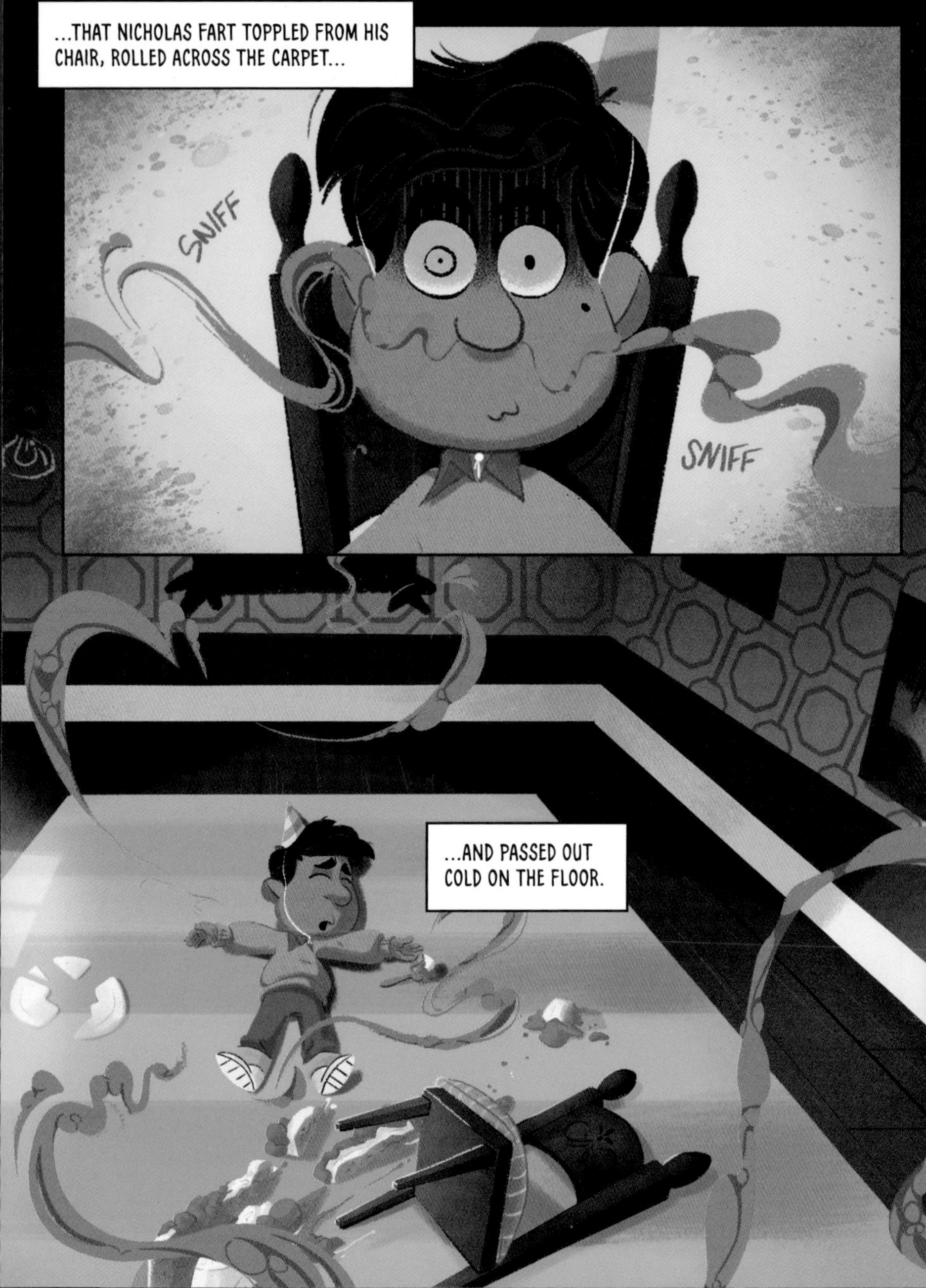
...THAT NICHOLAS FART TOPPLED FROM HIS CHAIR, ROLLED ACROSS THE CARPET...
SNIFF
SNIFF
...AND PASSED OUT COLD ON THE FLOOR.

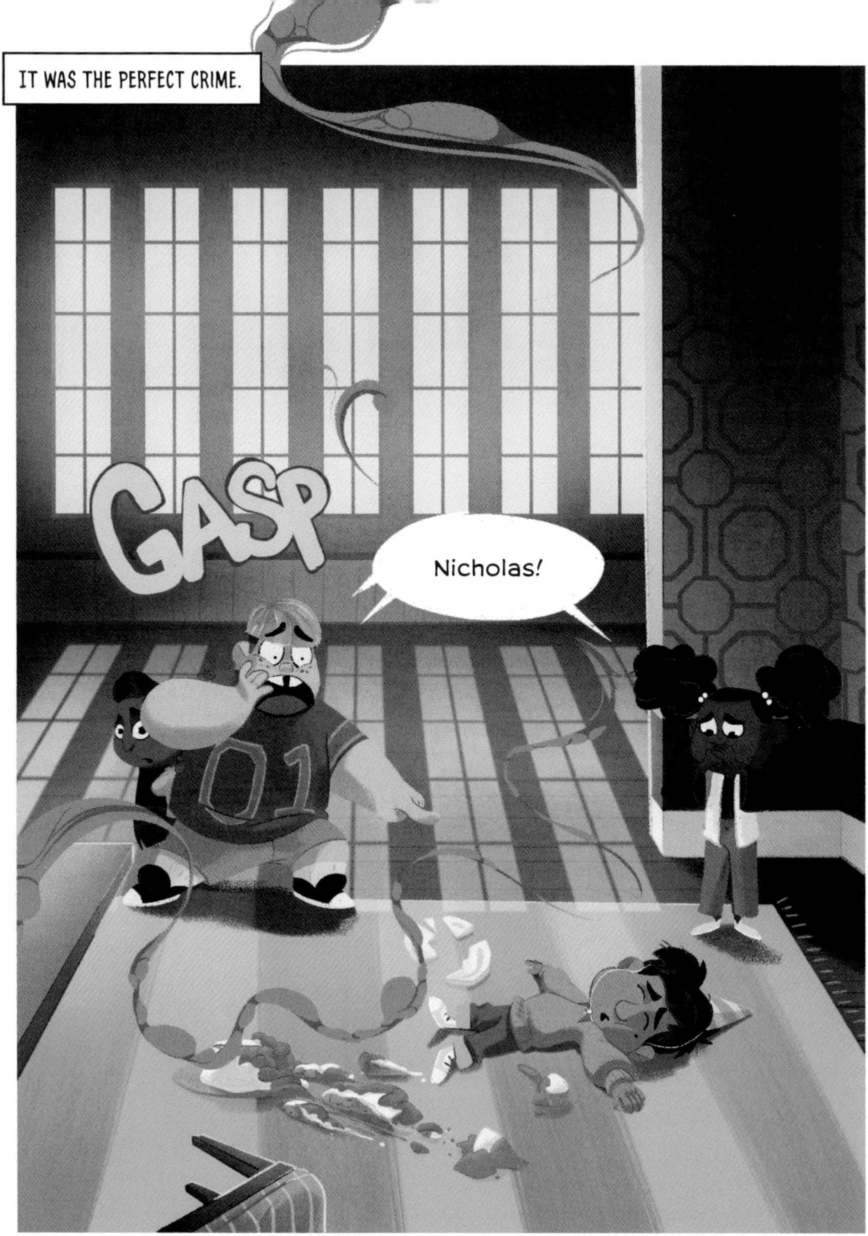
IT WAS THE PERFECT CRIME.
GASP
Nicholas!

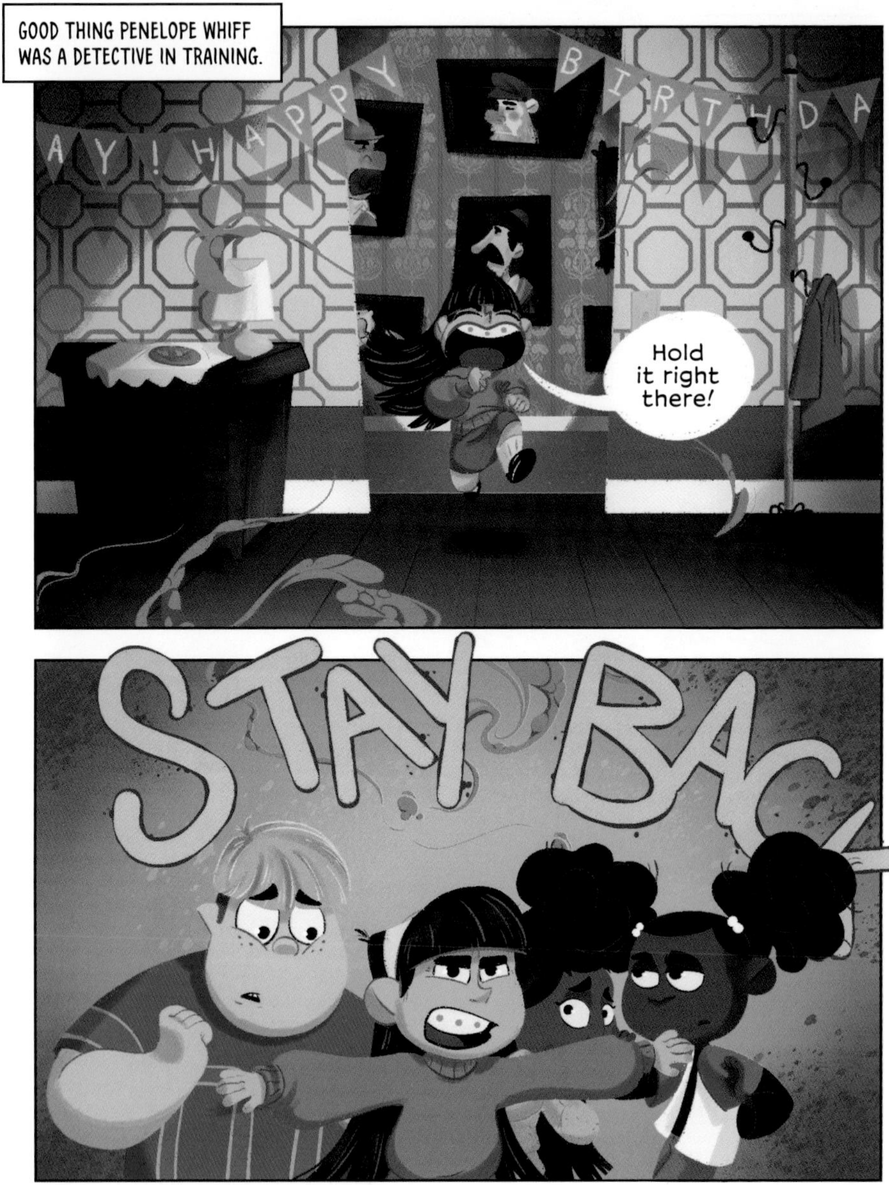
GOOD THING PENELOPE WHIFF WAS A DETECTIVE IN TRAINING.
AY! HAPPY BIRTHDA
Hold it right there!
STAY BAC

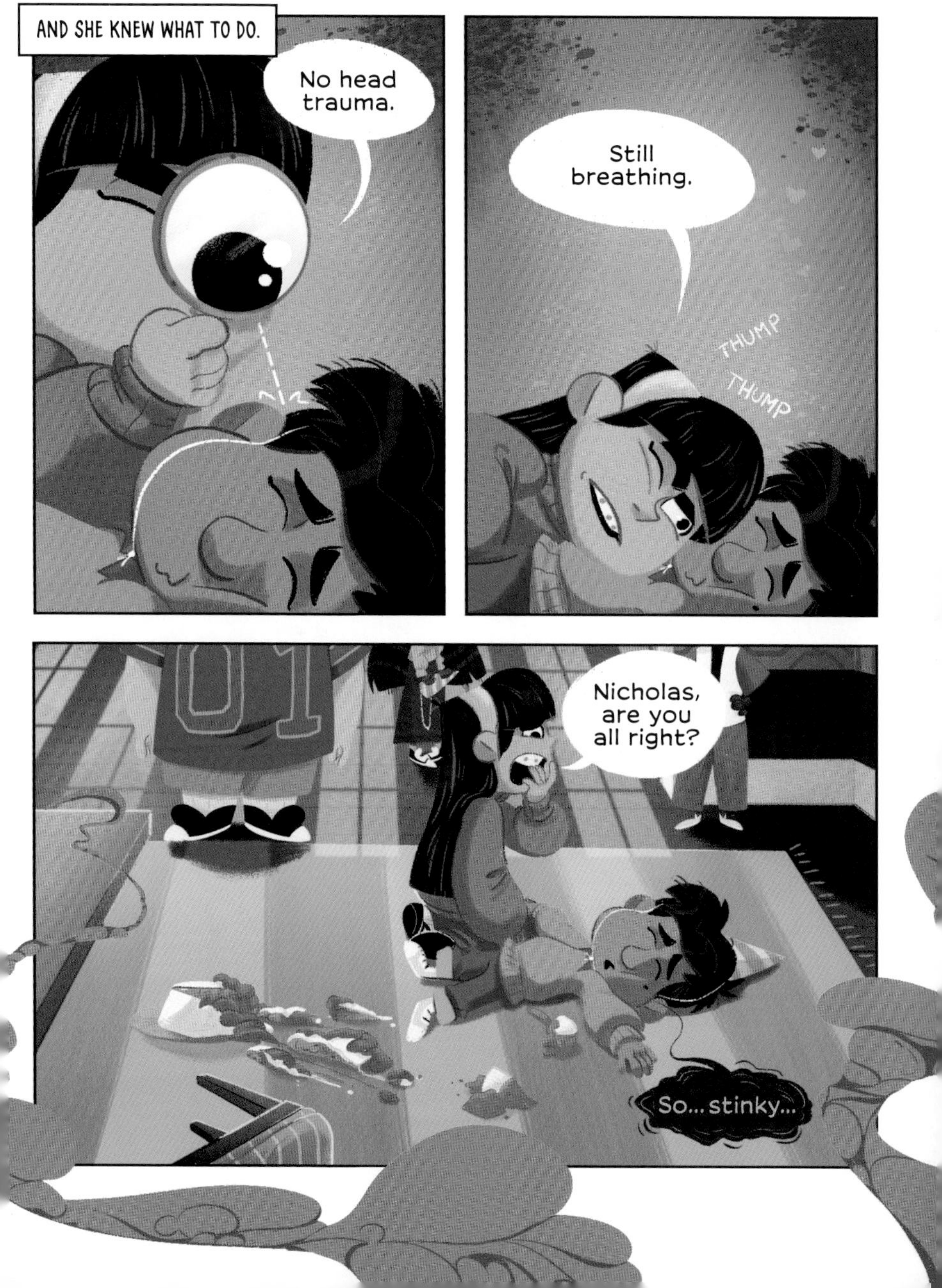
AND SHE KNEW WHAT TO DO.
No head trauma.
Still breathing.
THUMP
THUMP
Nicholas, are you all right?
So... stinky...

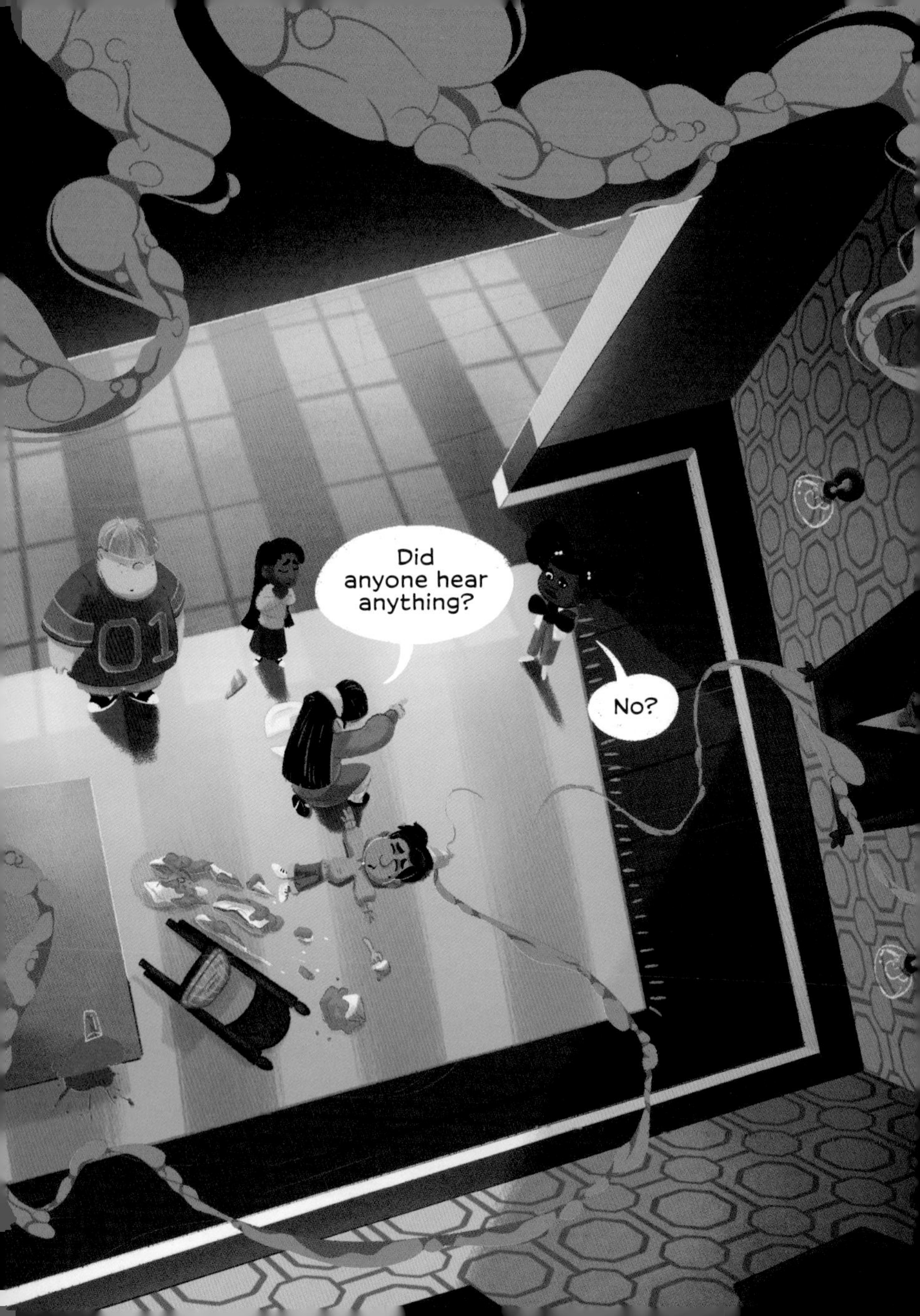

Did anyone hear anything?
No?

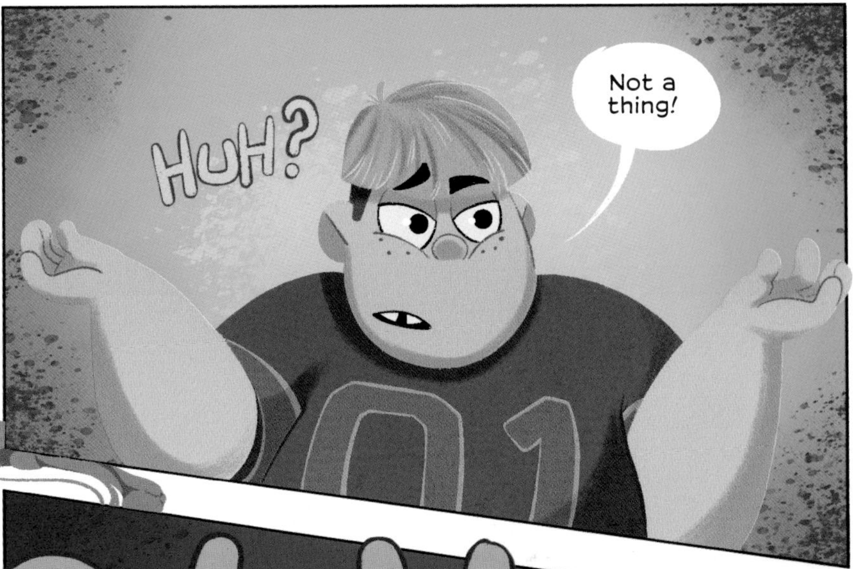
HUH?
Not a thing!
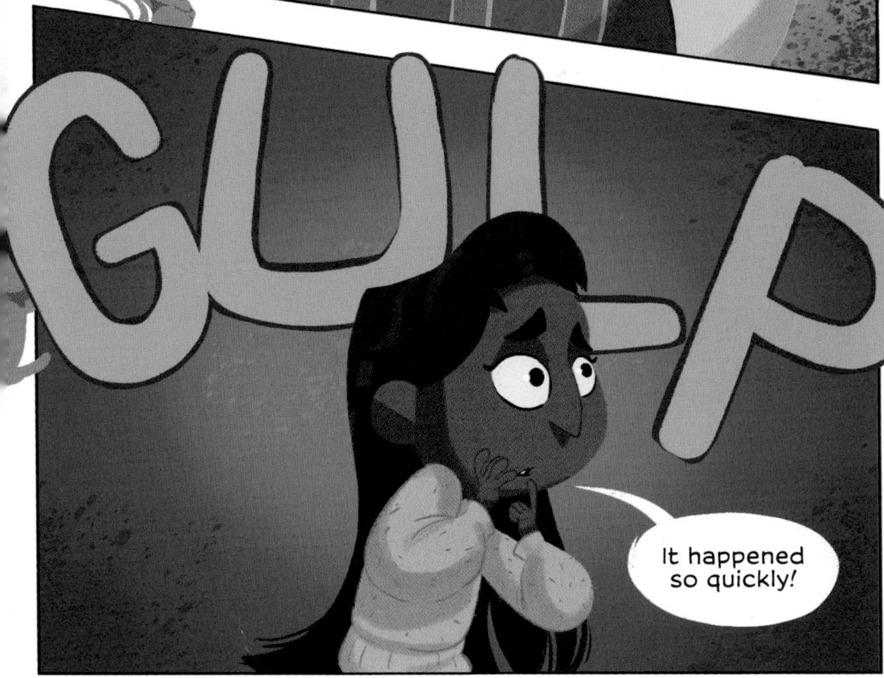
GULP
It happened so quickly!

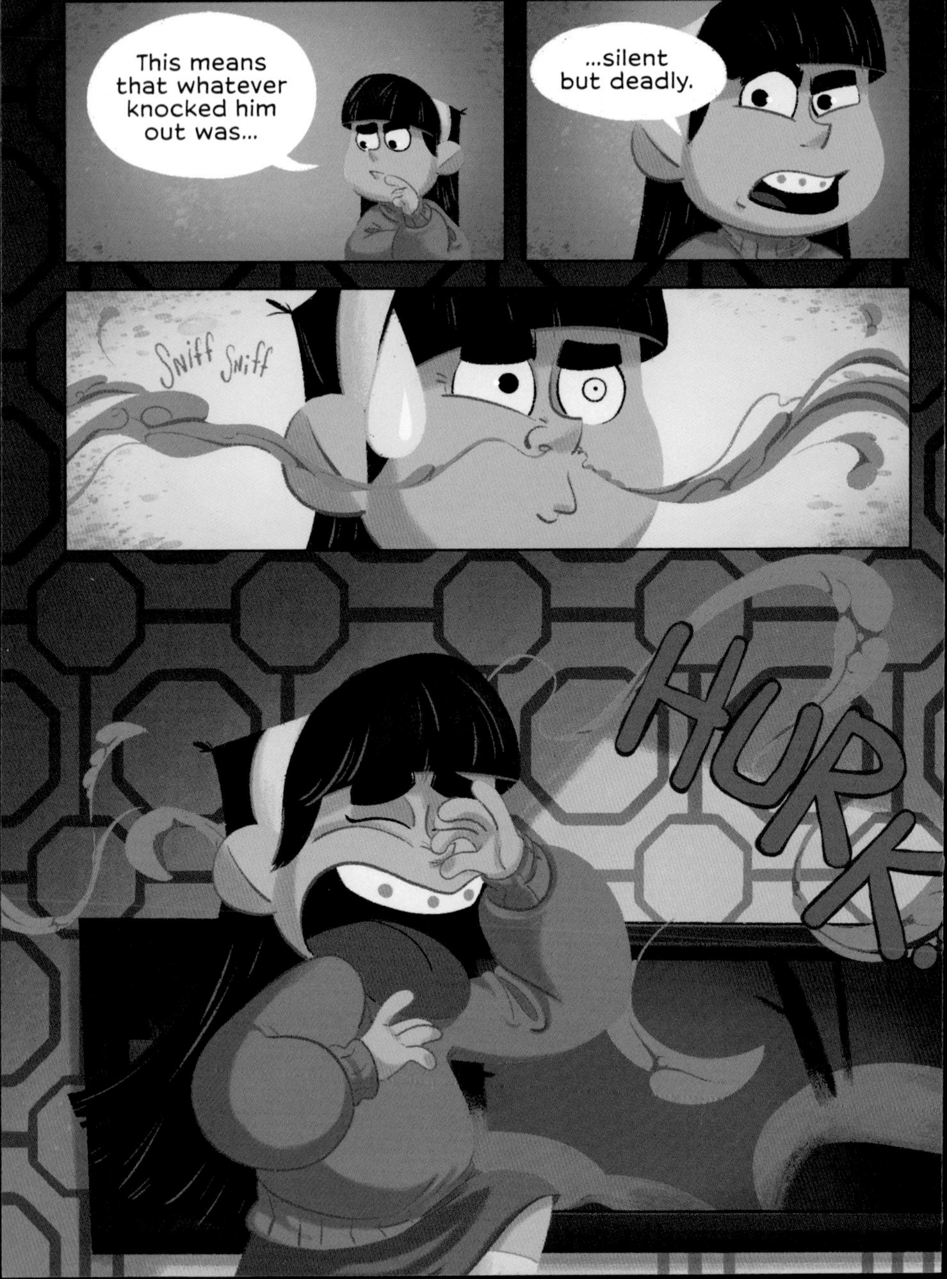
This means that whatever knocked him out was...
...silent but deadly.
SNIFF SNIFF
HURK!

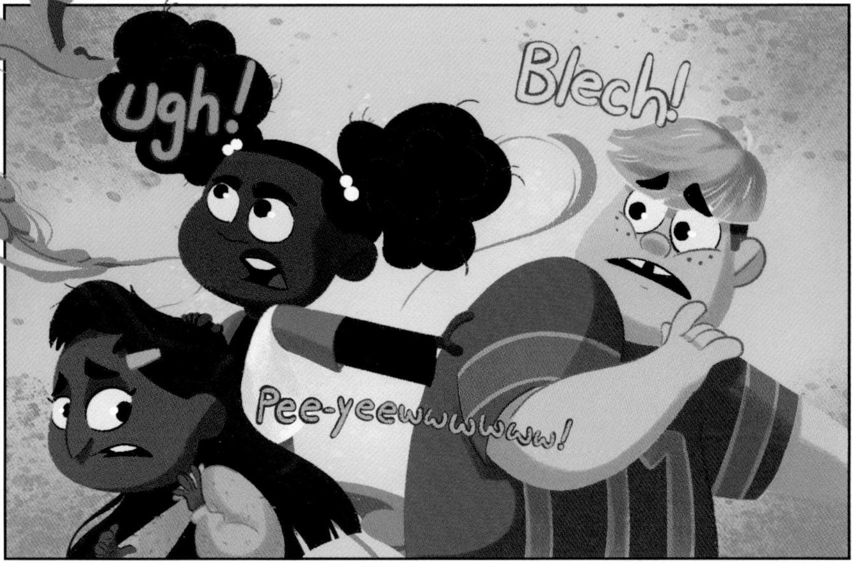
Ugh!
Blech!
Pee-yeewwwwwww!

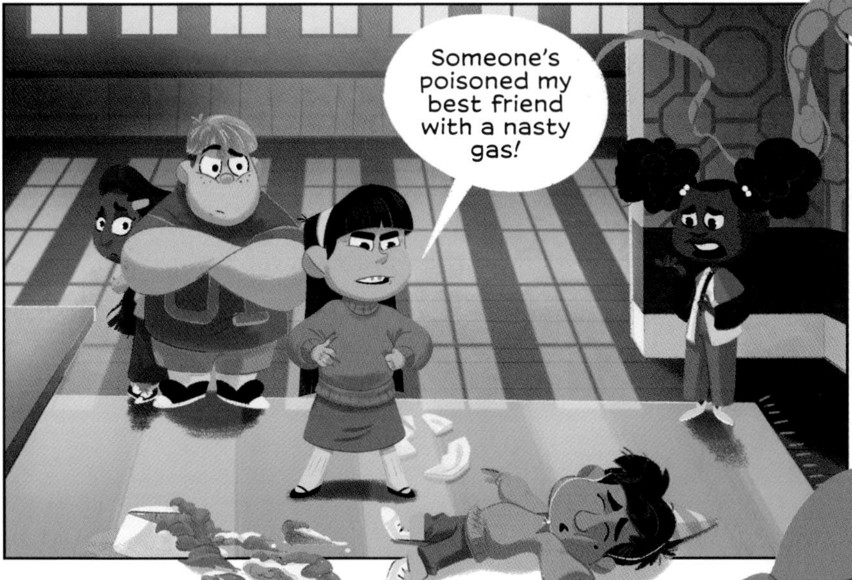
Someone's poisoned my best friend with a nasty gas!

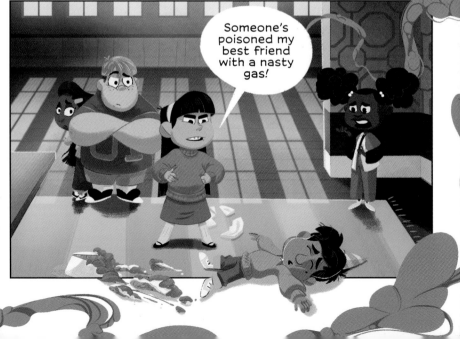

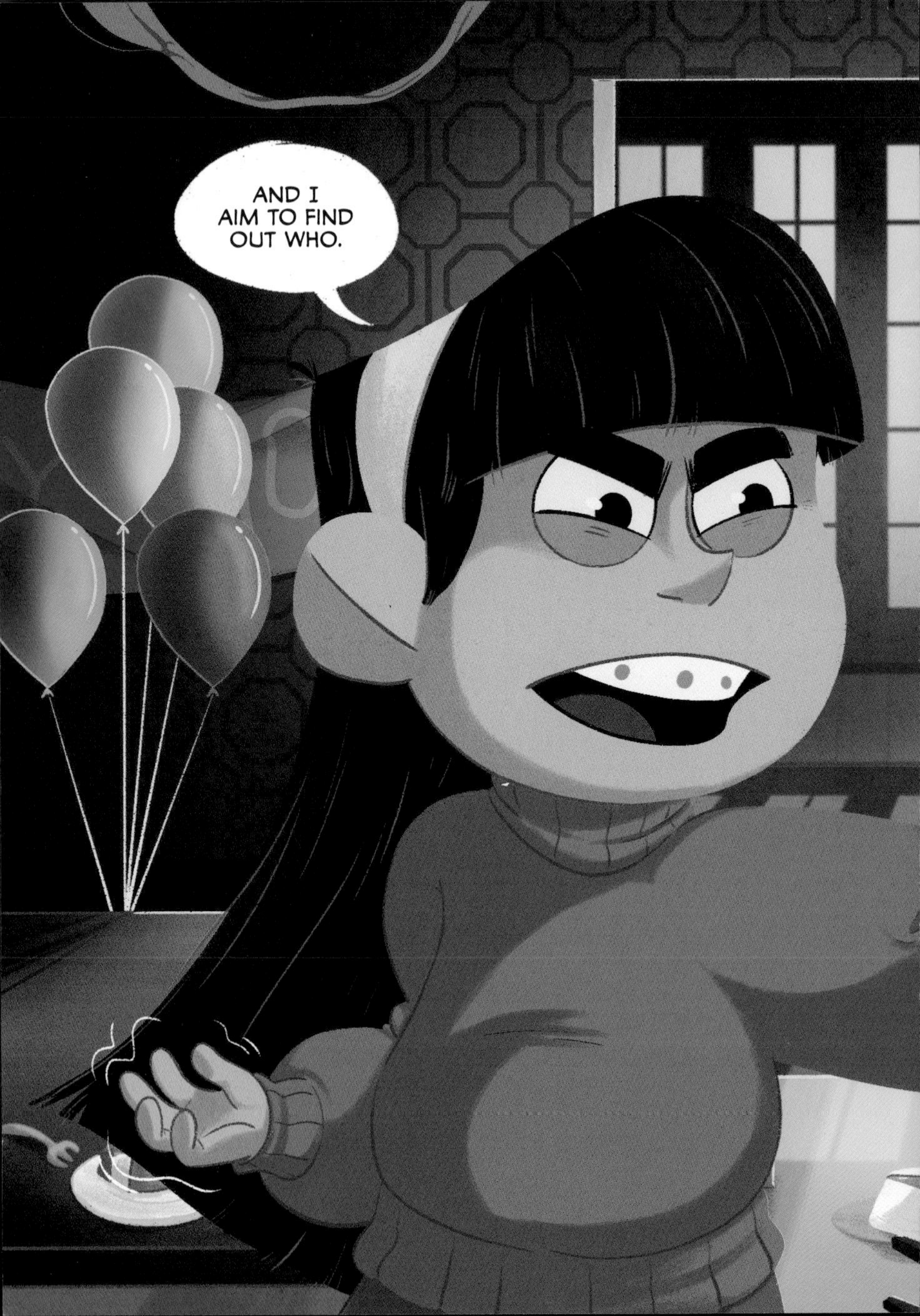
AND I AIM TO FIND OUT WHO.

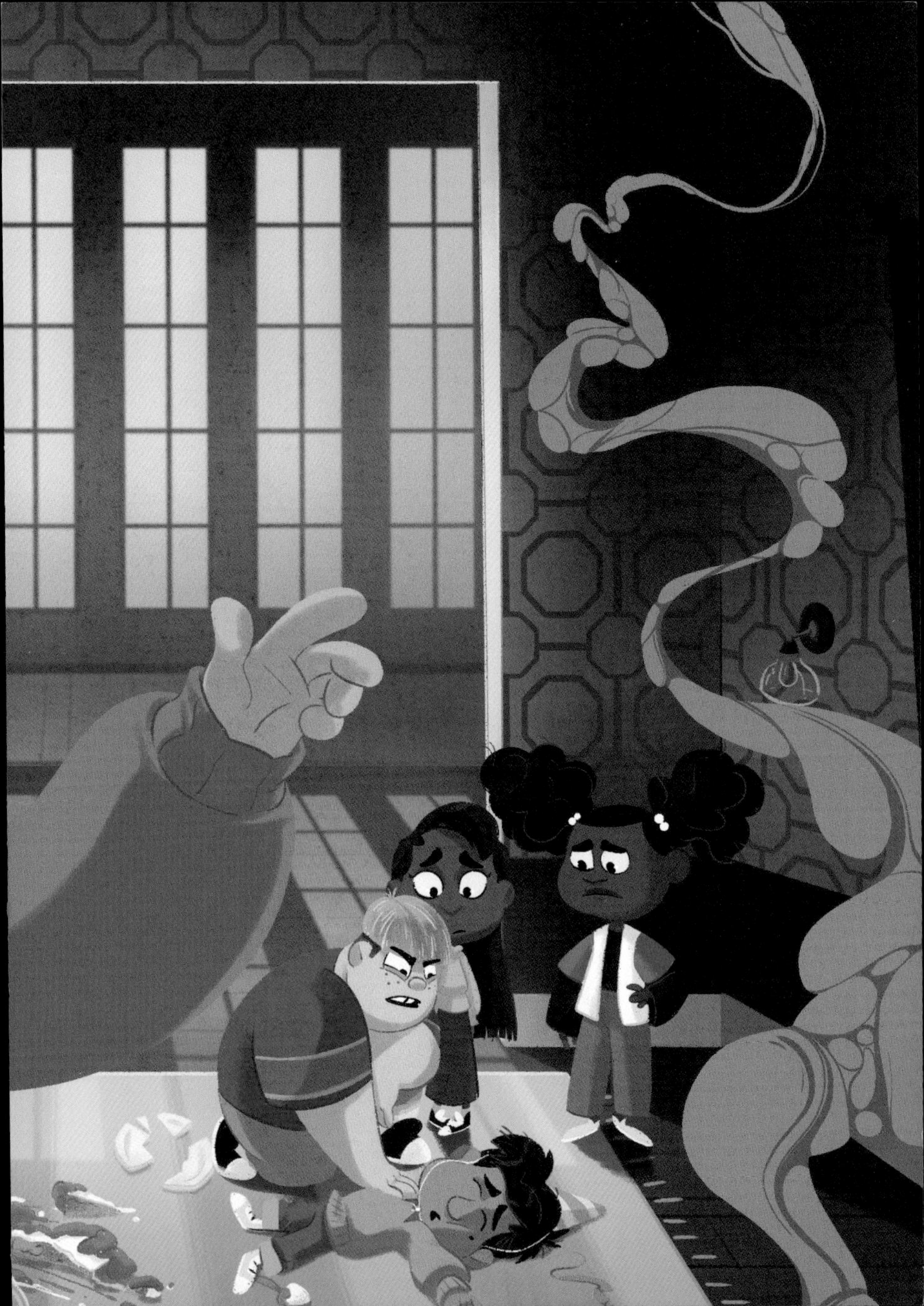

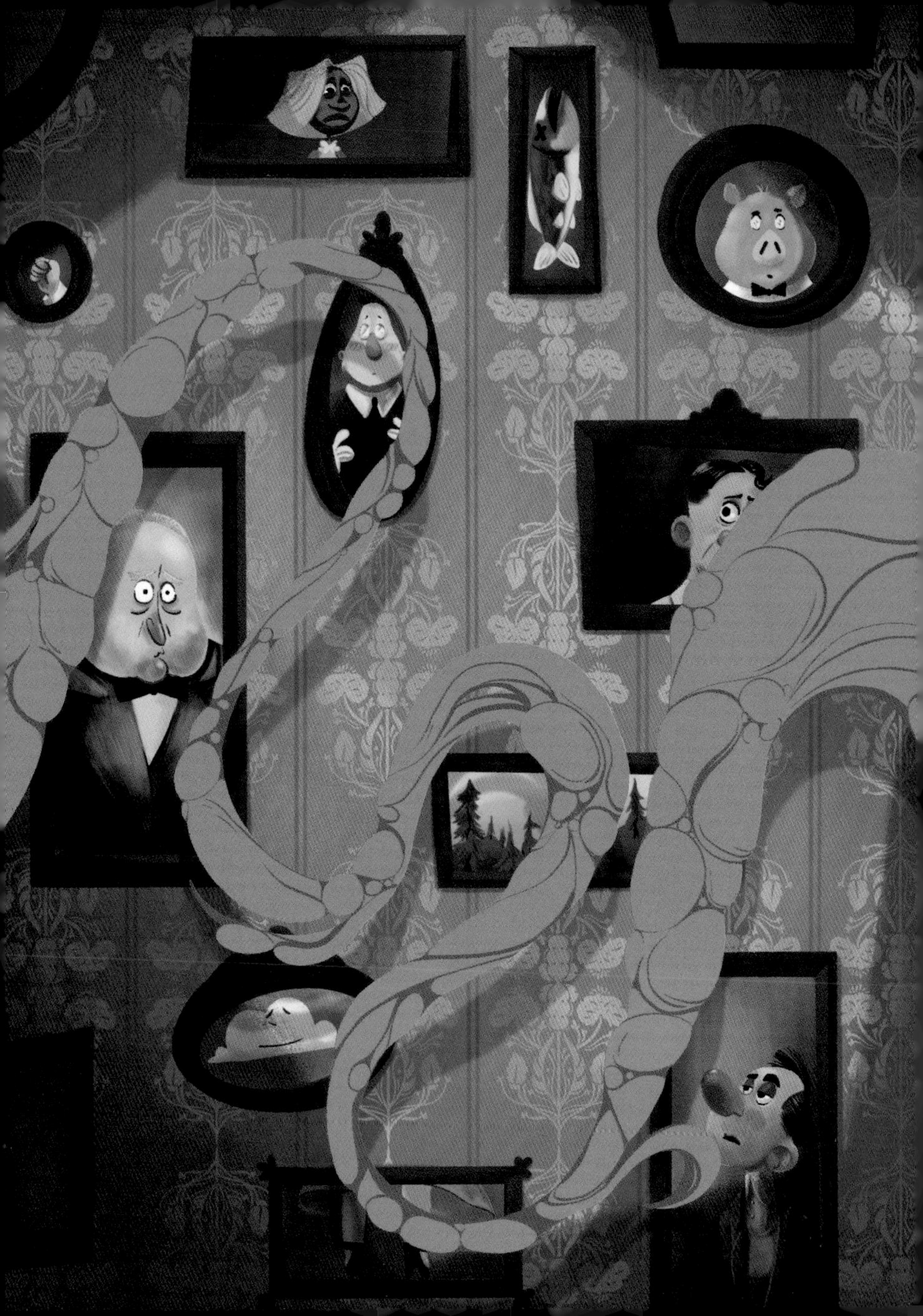

Chapter 2

SNIFFING OUT CLUES

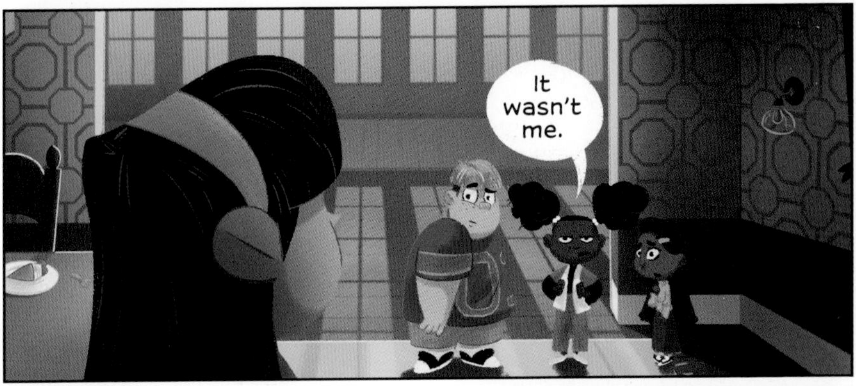
It wasn't me.

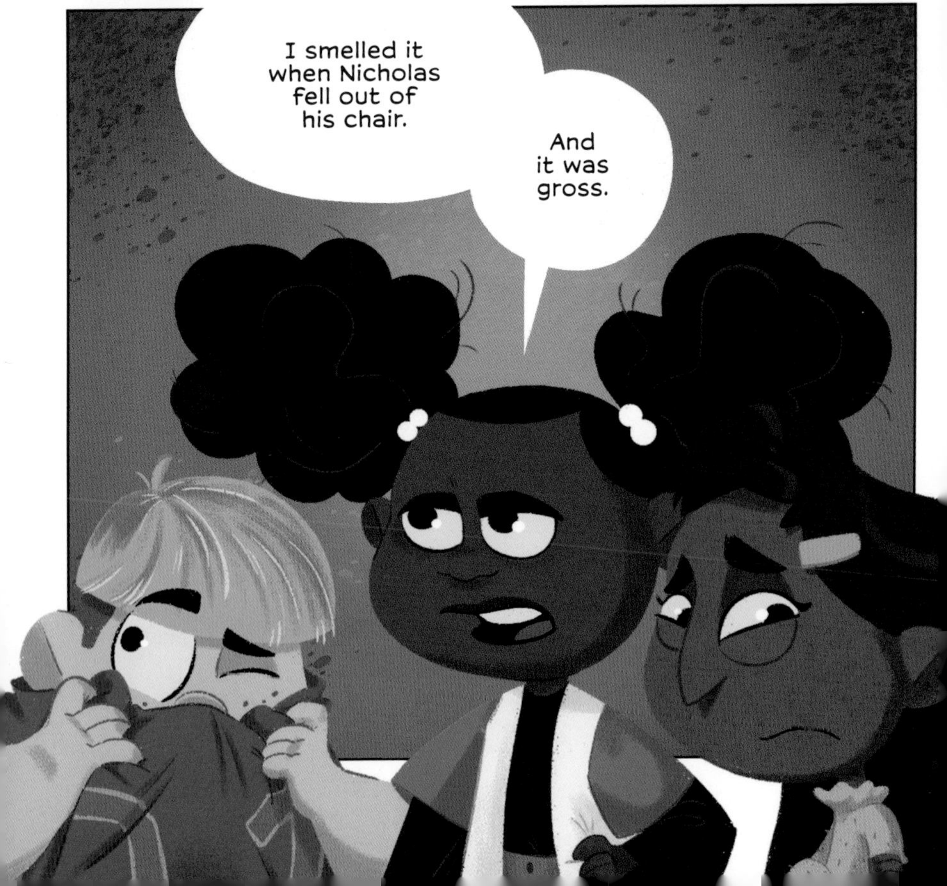
I smelled it when Nicholas fell out of his chair.
And it was gross.

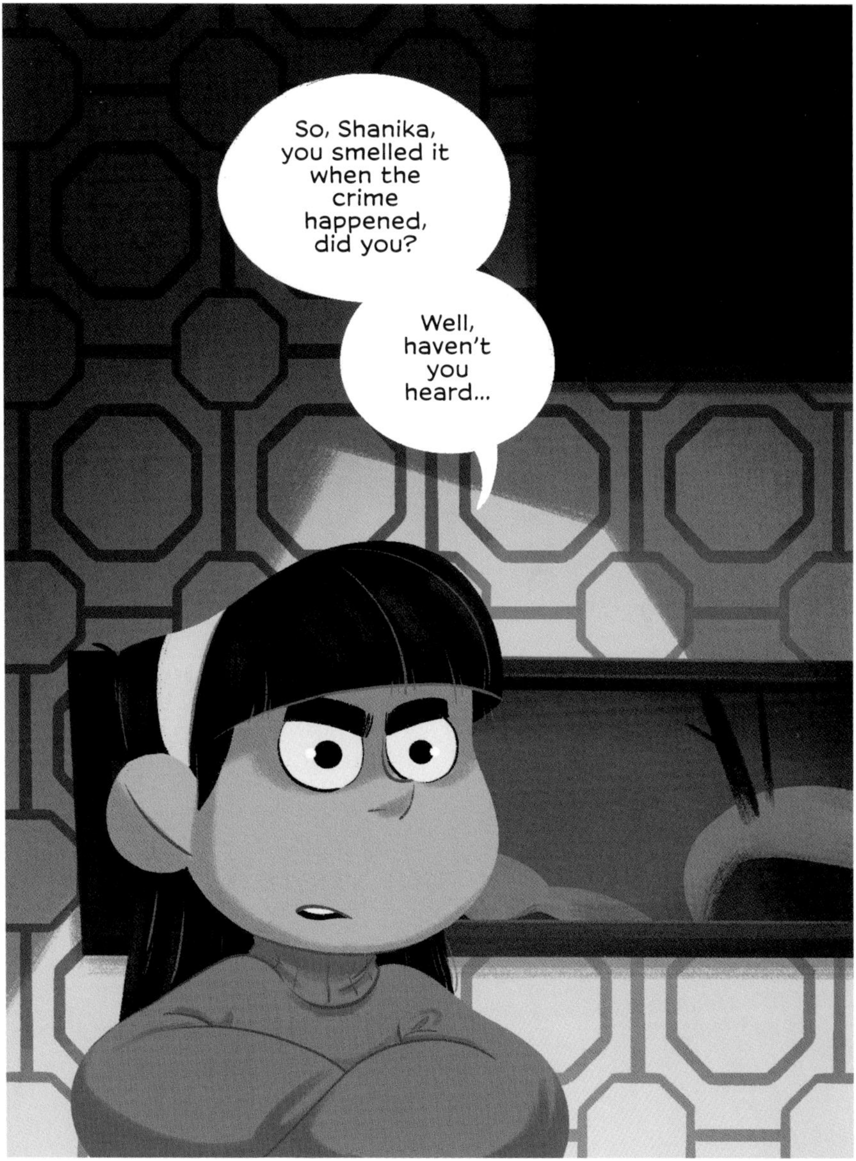
So, Shanika, you smelled it when the crime happened, did you?
Well, haven't you heard...

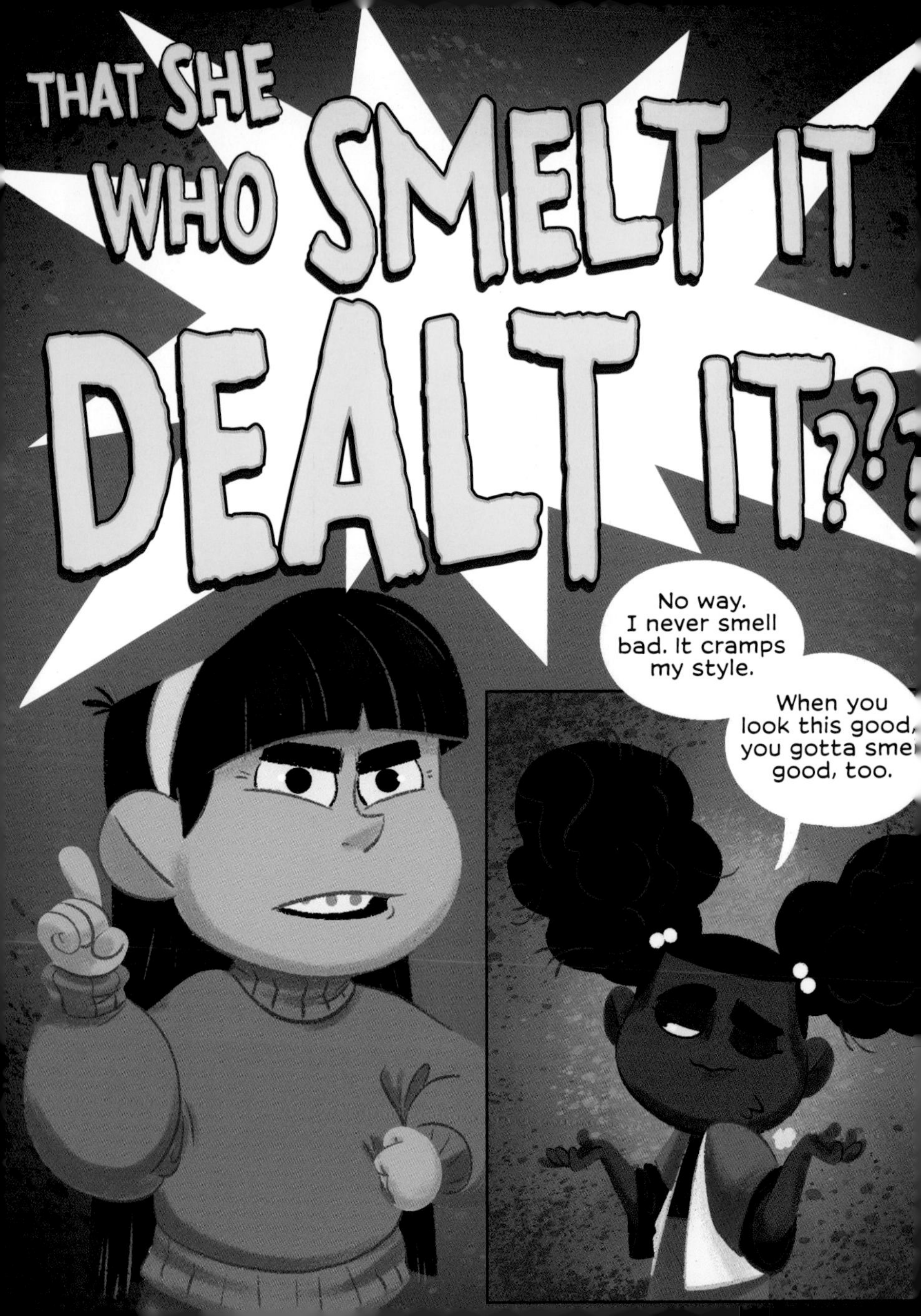
THAT SHE WHO SMELT IT DEALT IT??
No way. I never smell bad. It cramps my style.
When you look this good, you gotta sme
good, too.

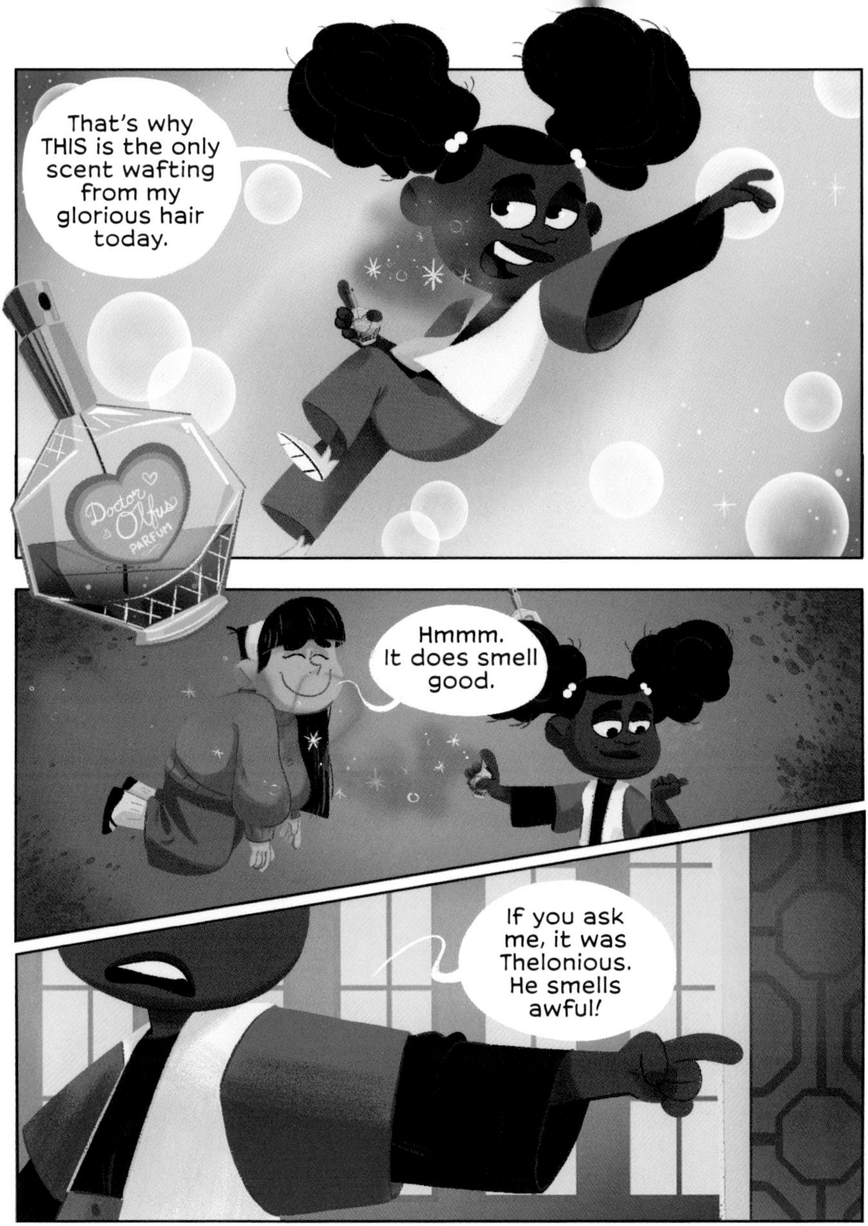
That's why THIS is the only scent wafting from my glorious hair today.
Doctor Olfus PARFUM
Hmmm. It does smell good.
If you ask me, it was Thelonious. He smells awful!

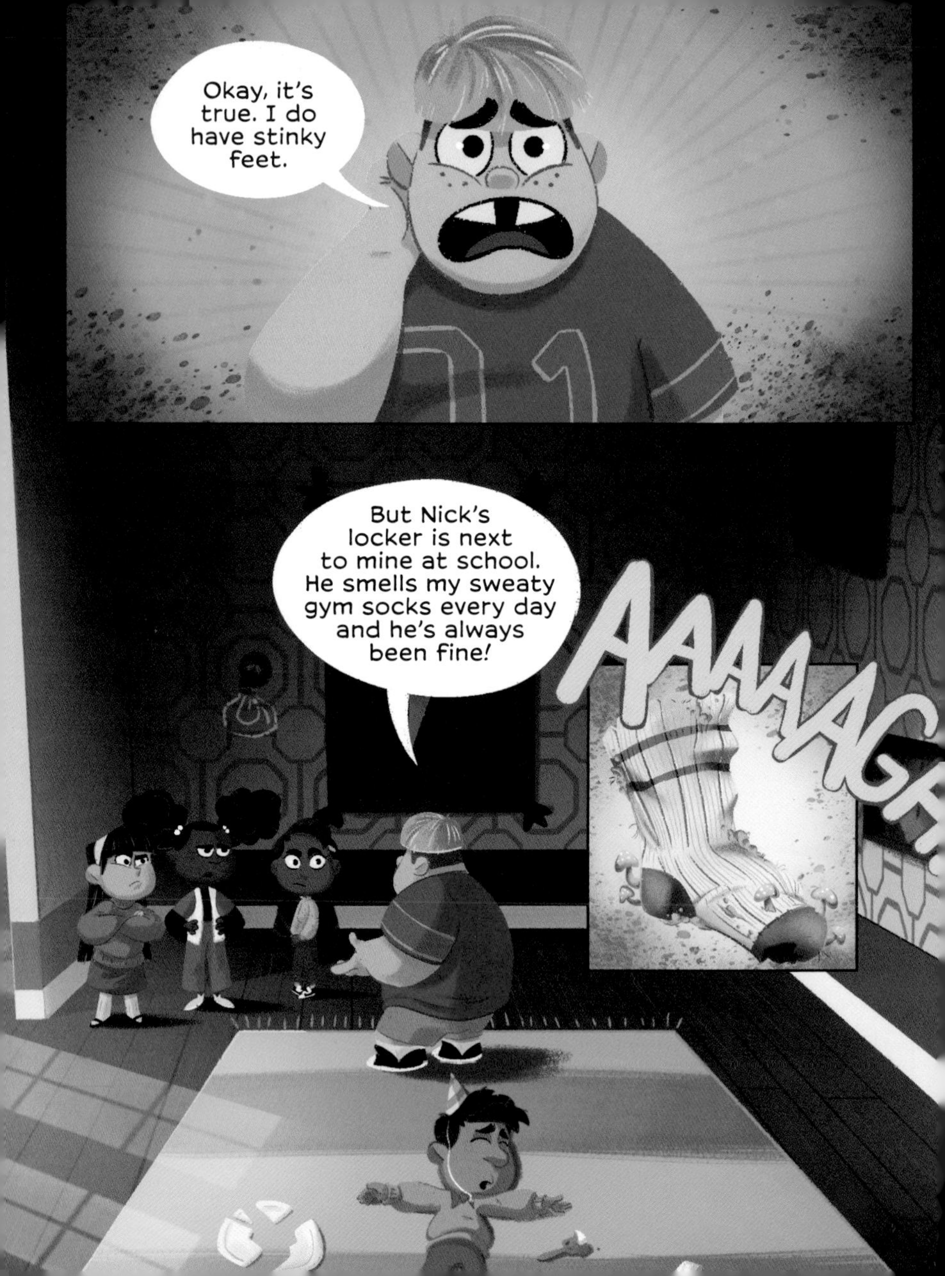
Okay, it's true. I do have stinky feet.
But Nick's locker is next to mine at school. He smells my sweaty gym socks every day and he's always been fine!
AAAAAGH!

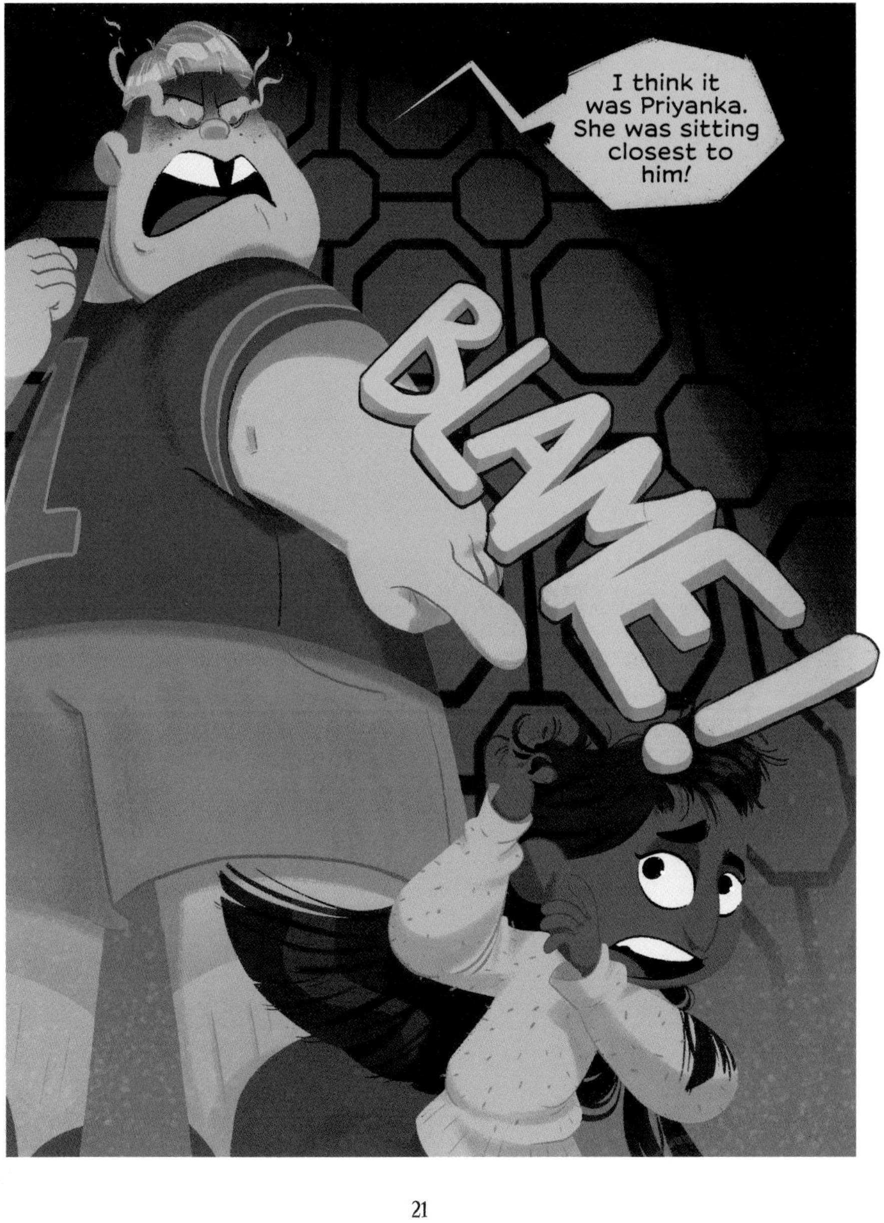
I think it was Priyanka. She was sitting closest to him!
BLAME!

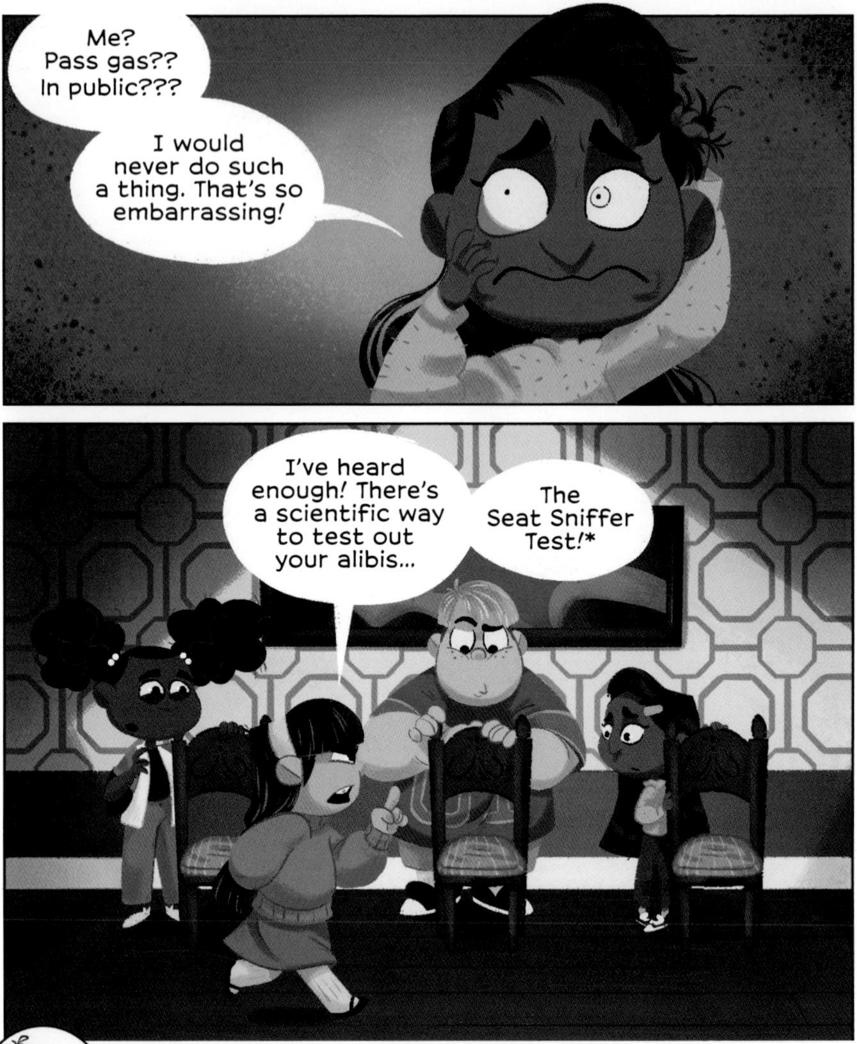
Me?
Pass gas??
In public???
I would never do such a thing. That's so embarrassing!
I've heard enough! There's a scientific way to test out your alibis...
The Seat Sniffer Test!*

S. GLUM

*THE SEAT SNIFFER TEST IS A FAMOUS DETECTIVE TRICK FIRST USED BY THE GREAT BELGIAN SLEUTH HERCULE POTTY TO SOLVE THE CASE OF THE DISAPPEARING DOO-DOO. IT IS THE SECOND THING STUDENTS LEARN IN DETECTIVE SCHOOL, BETWEEN (1) USING A MAGNIFYING GLASS AND (3) BEING SERIOUS.

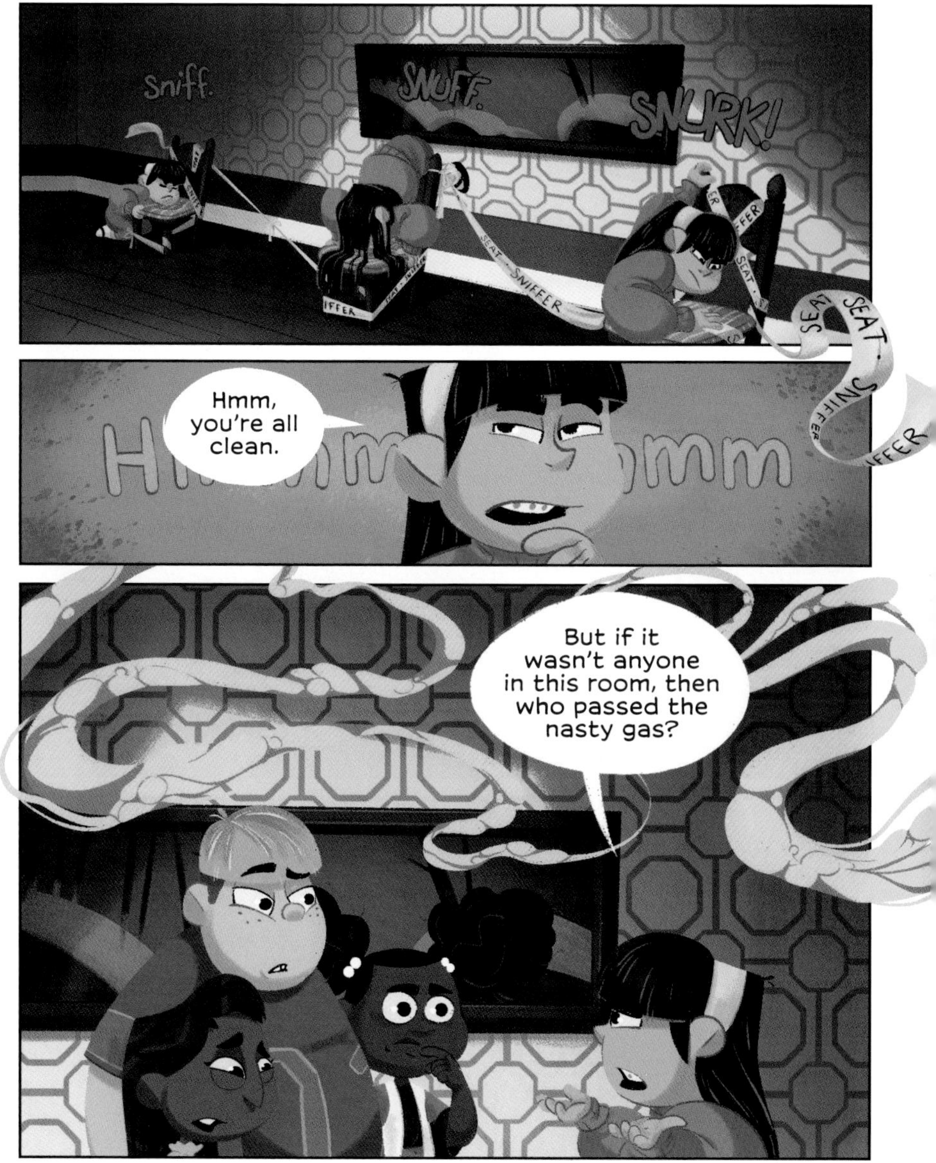
sniff.
SNUFF.
SNURK!
SEAT SNIFFER
Hmm, you're all clean.
But if it wasn't anyone in this room, then who passed the nasty gas?

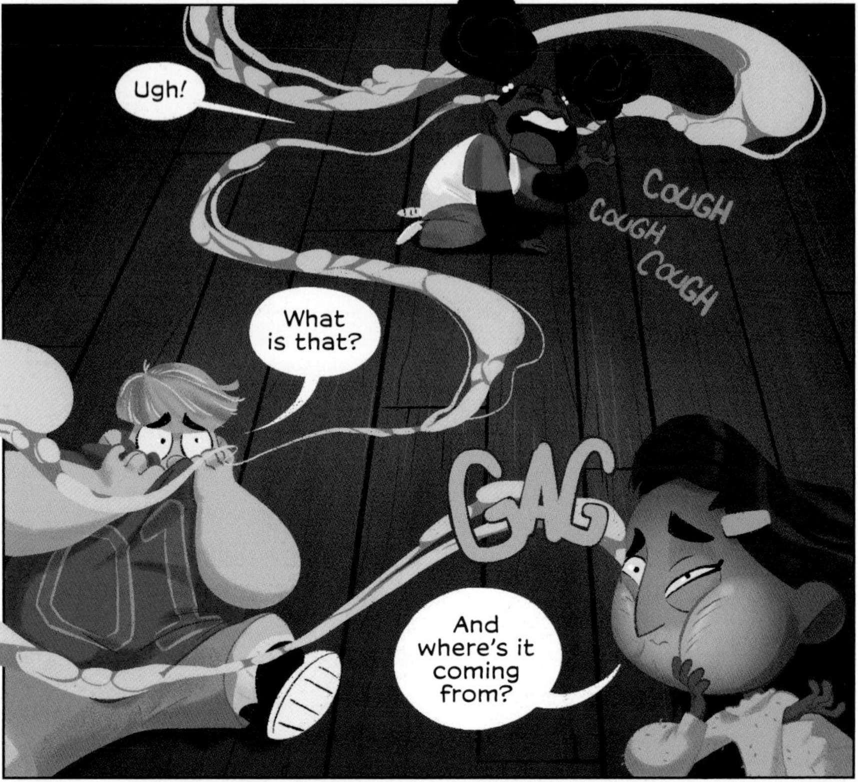
Ugh!
COUGH COUGH COUGH
What is that?
GAG
And where's it coming from?

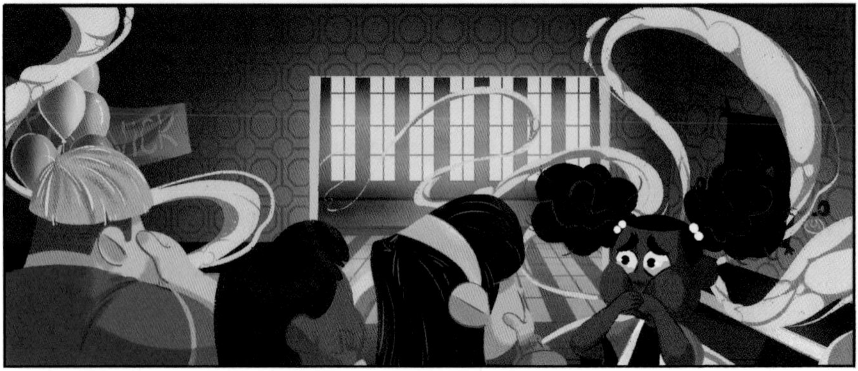

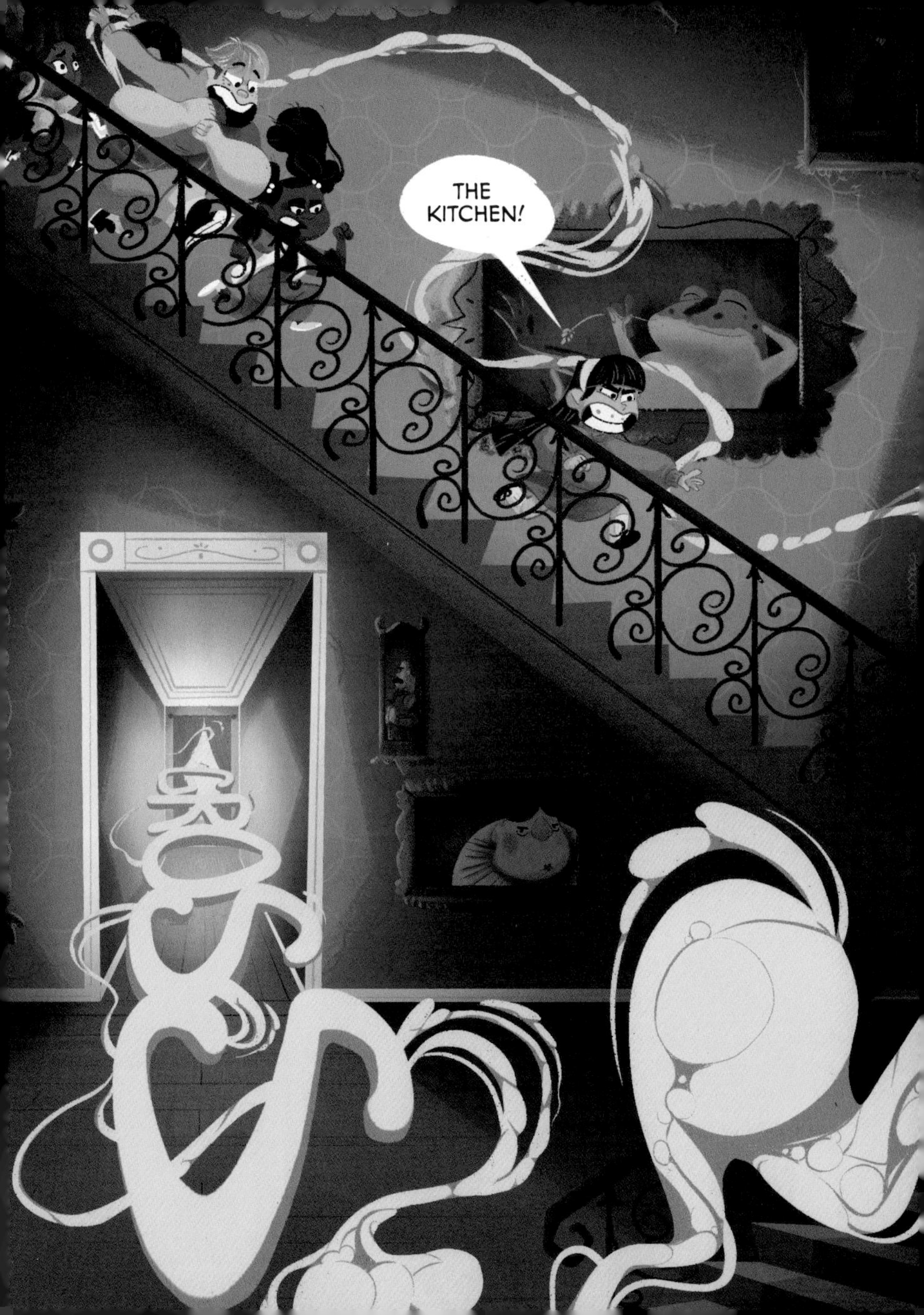
THE KITCHEN!

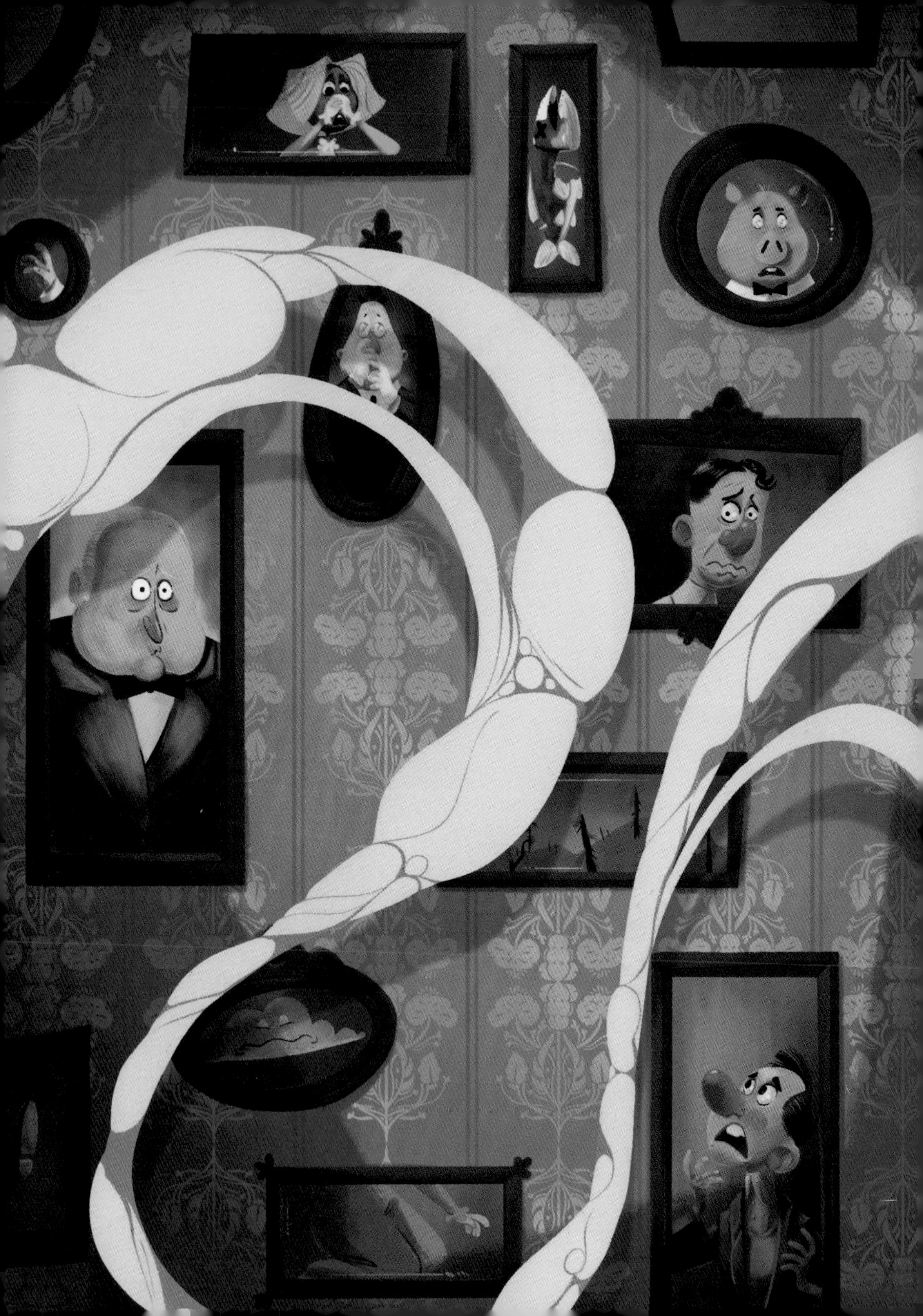

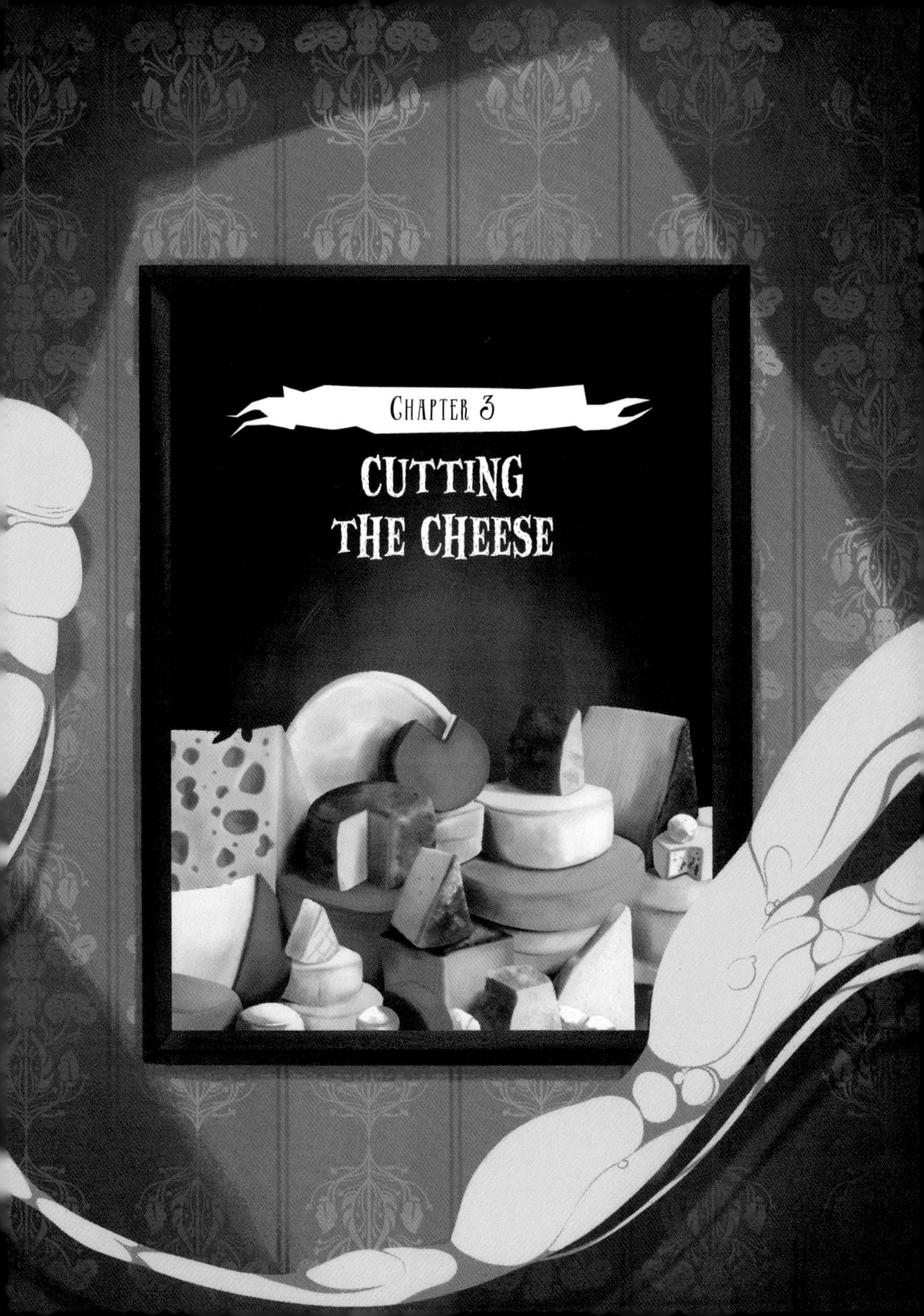
CHAPTER 3
CUTTING THE CHEESE

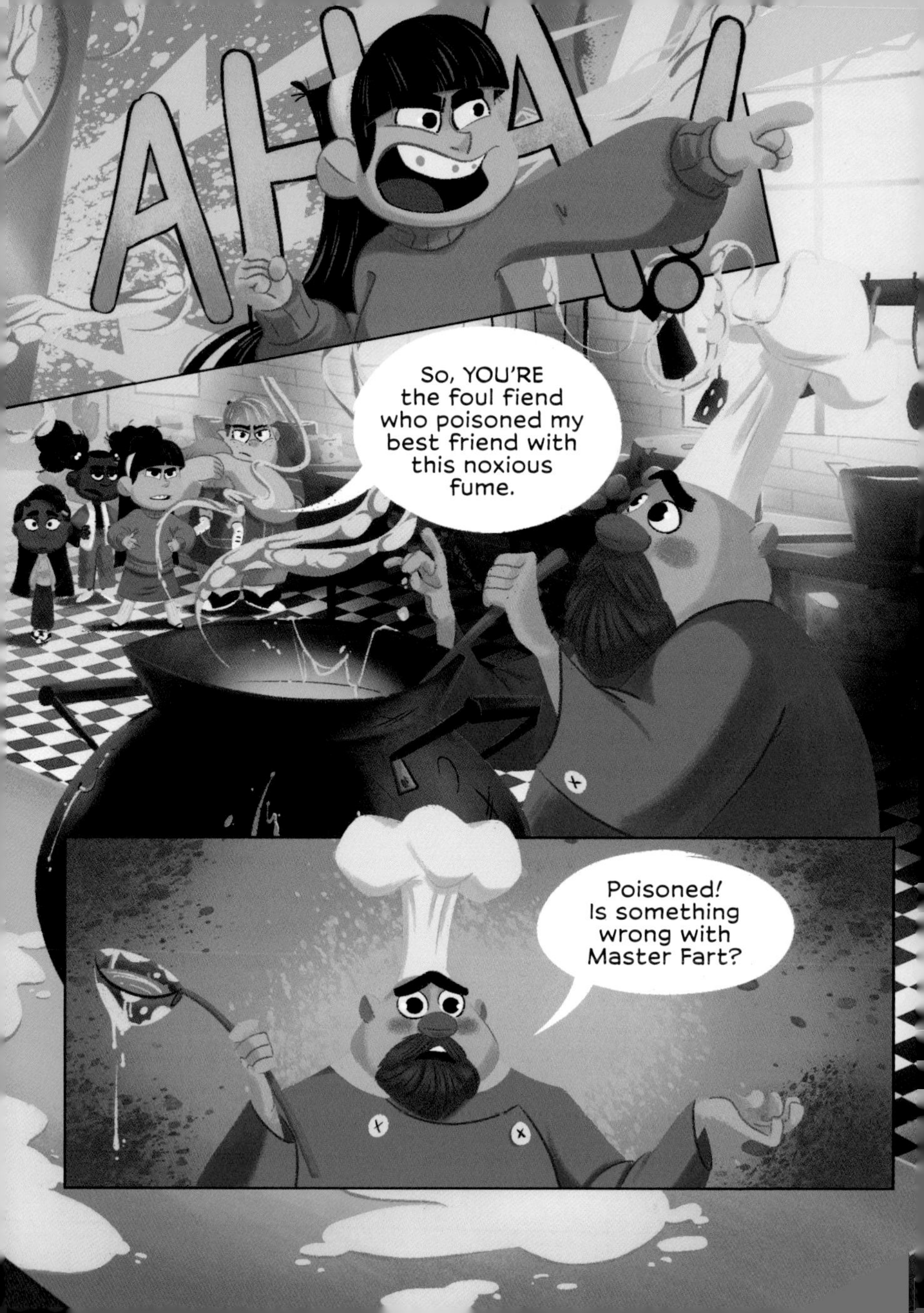
AHA!
So, YOU'RE the foul fiend who poisoned my best friend with this noxious fume.
Poisoned! Is something wrong with Master Fart?

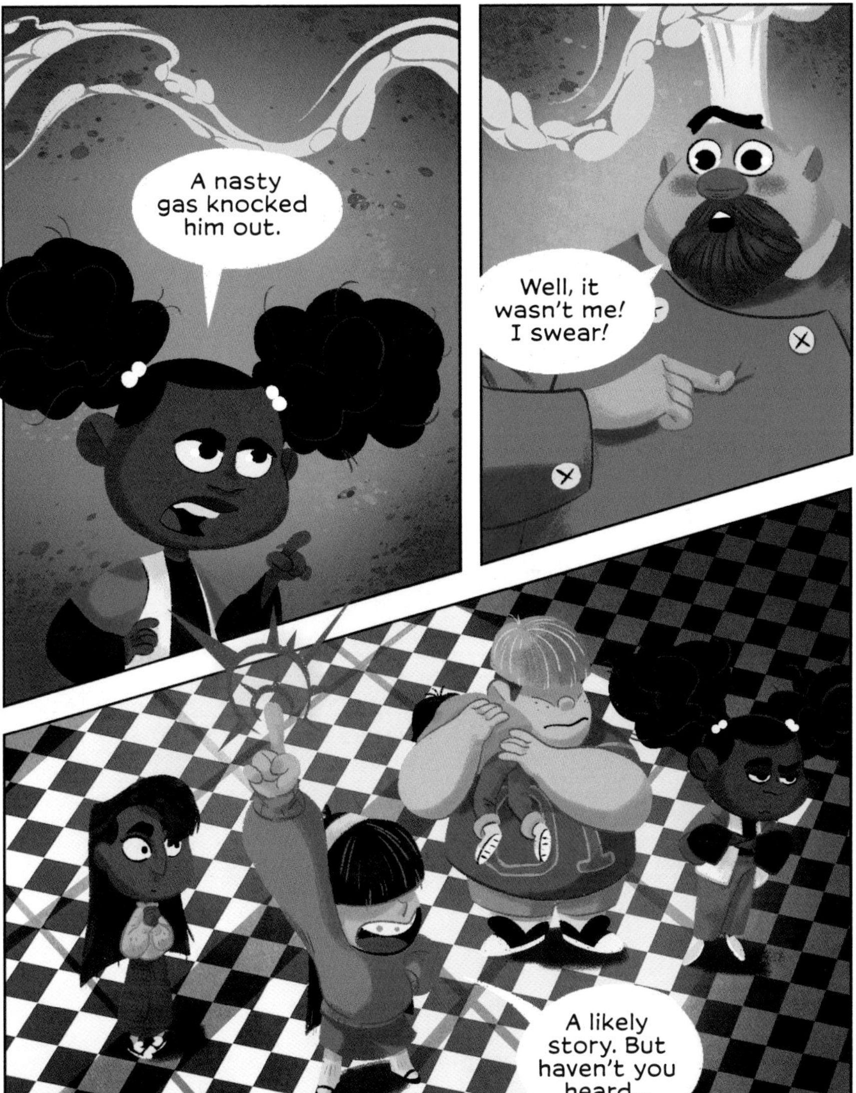
A nasty gas knocked him out.
Well, it wasn't me! I swear!
A likely story. But haven't you heard...

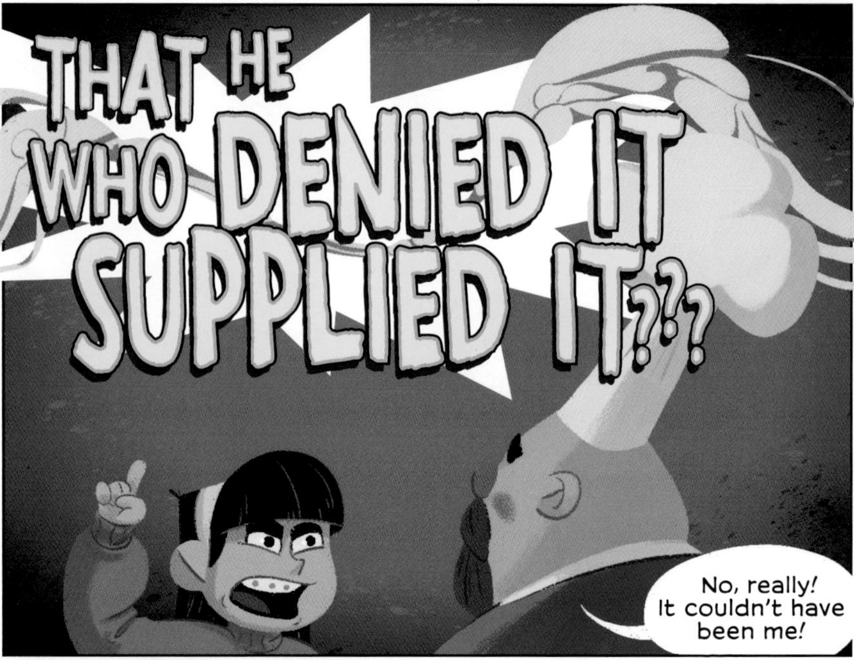
THAT HE WHO DENIED IT SUPPLIED IT???
No, really! It couldn't have been me!

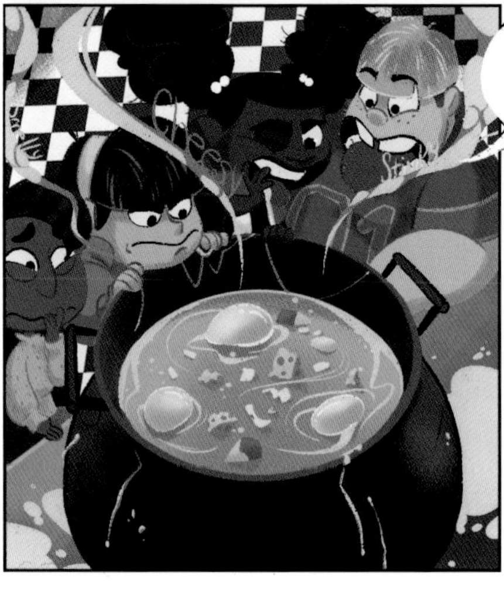
Then what's that?

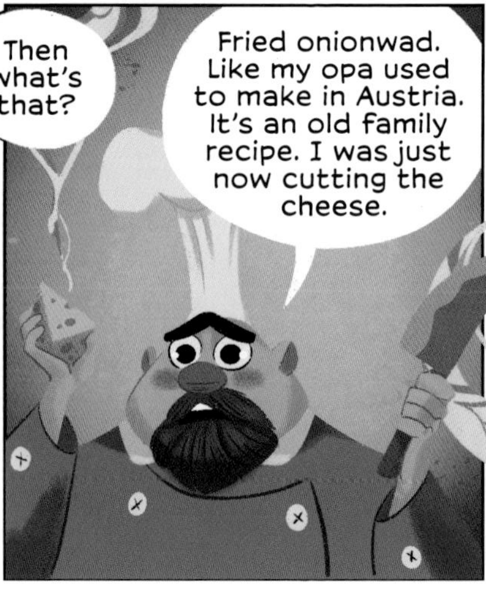
Fried onionwad. Like my opa used to make in Austria. It's an old family recipe. I was just now cutting the cheese.

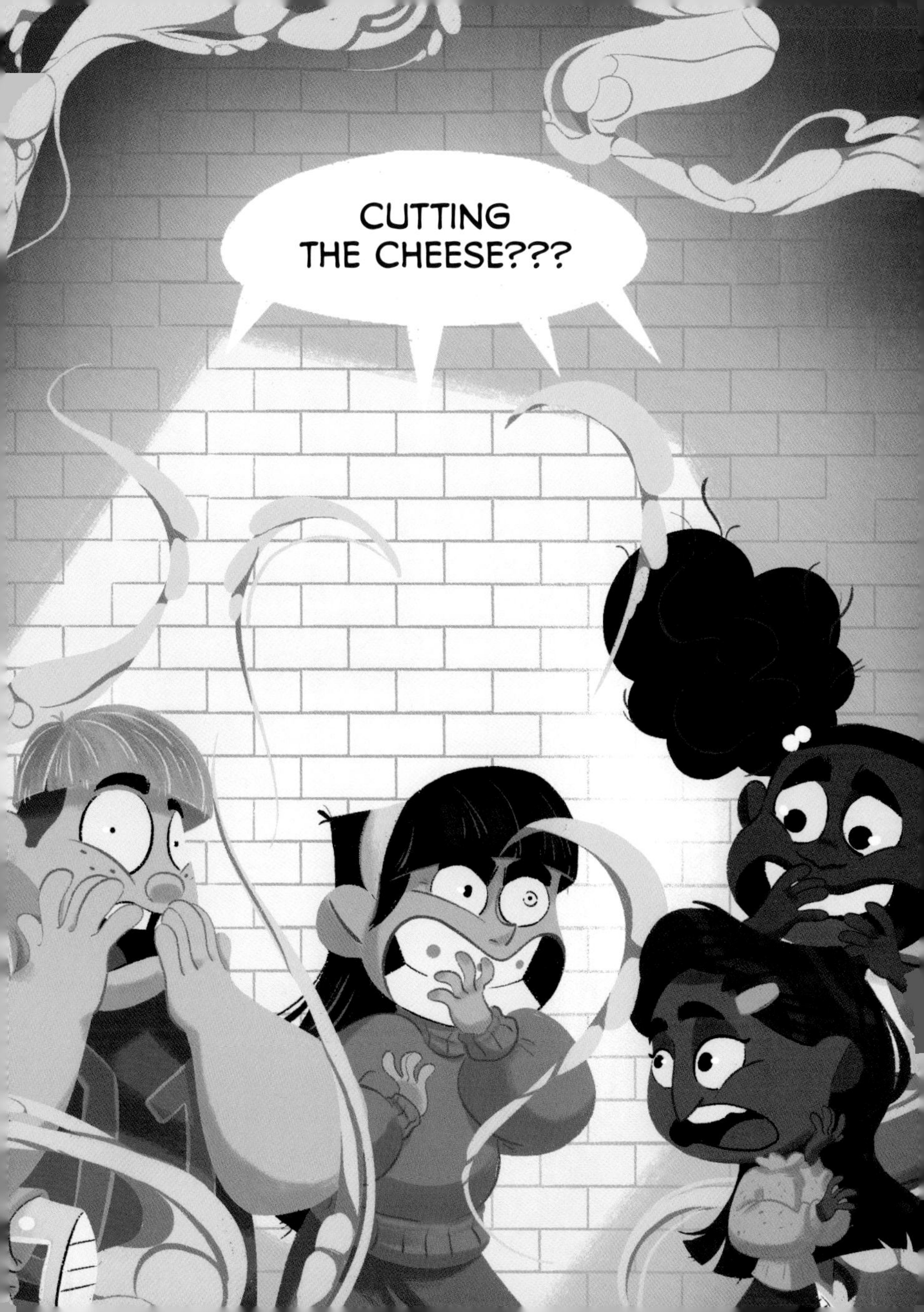
CUTTING THE CHEESE???

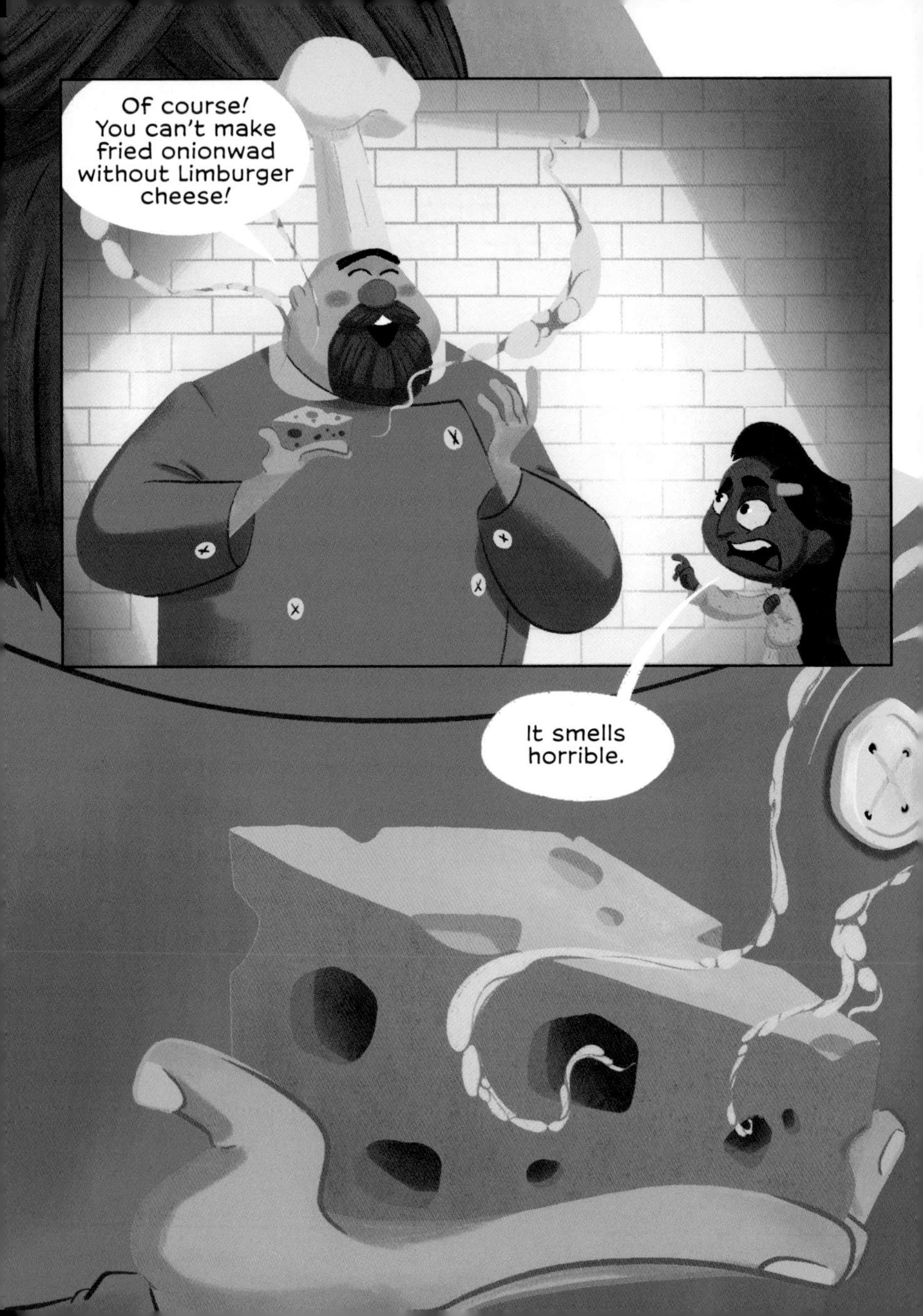
Of course! You can't make fried onionwad without Limburger cheese!
It smells horrible.

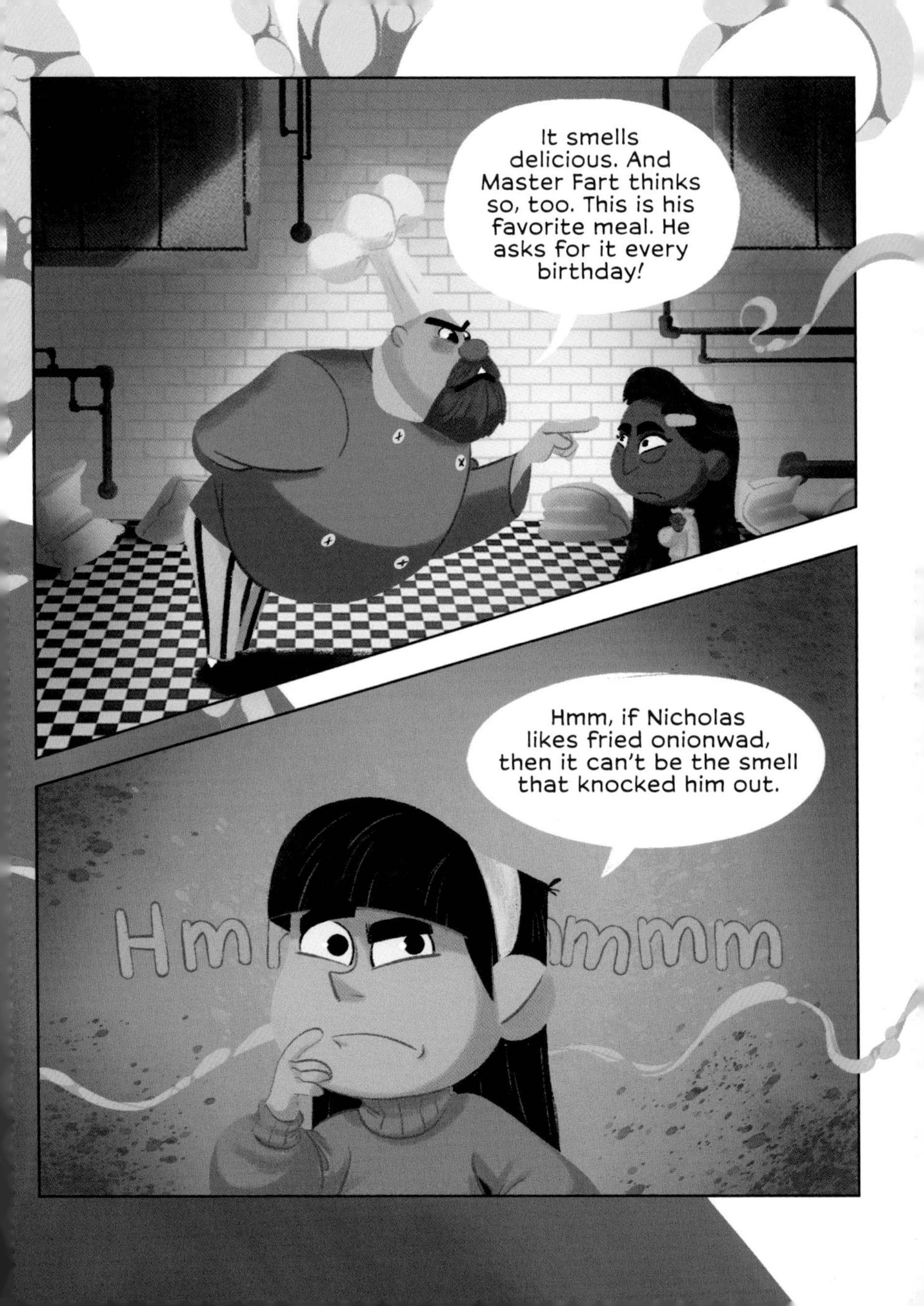
It smells delicious. And Master Fart thinks so, too. This is his favorite meal. He asks for it every birthday!
Hmm, if Nicholas likes fried onionwad, then it can't be the smell that knocked him out.

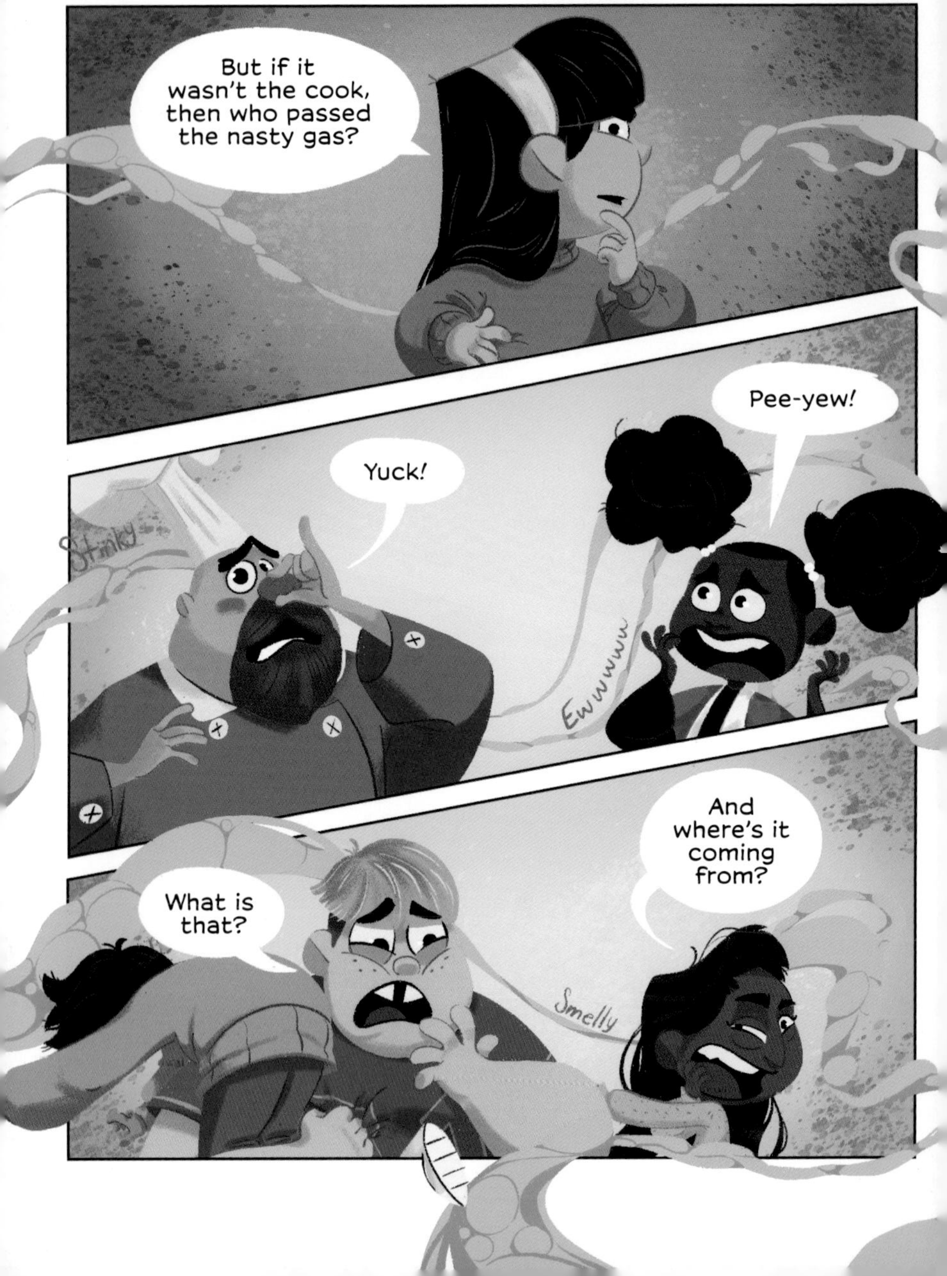
But if it wasn't the cook, then who passed the nasty gas?
Yuck!
Pee-yew!
Stinky
Ewwwww
What is that?
And where's it coming from?
Smelly

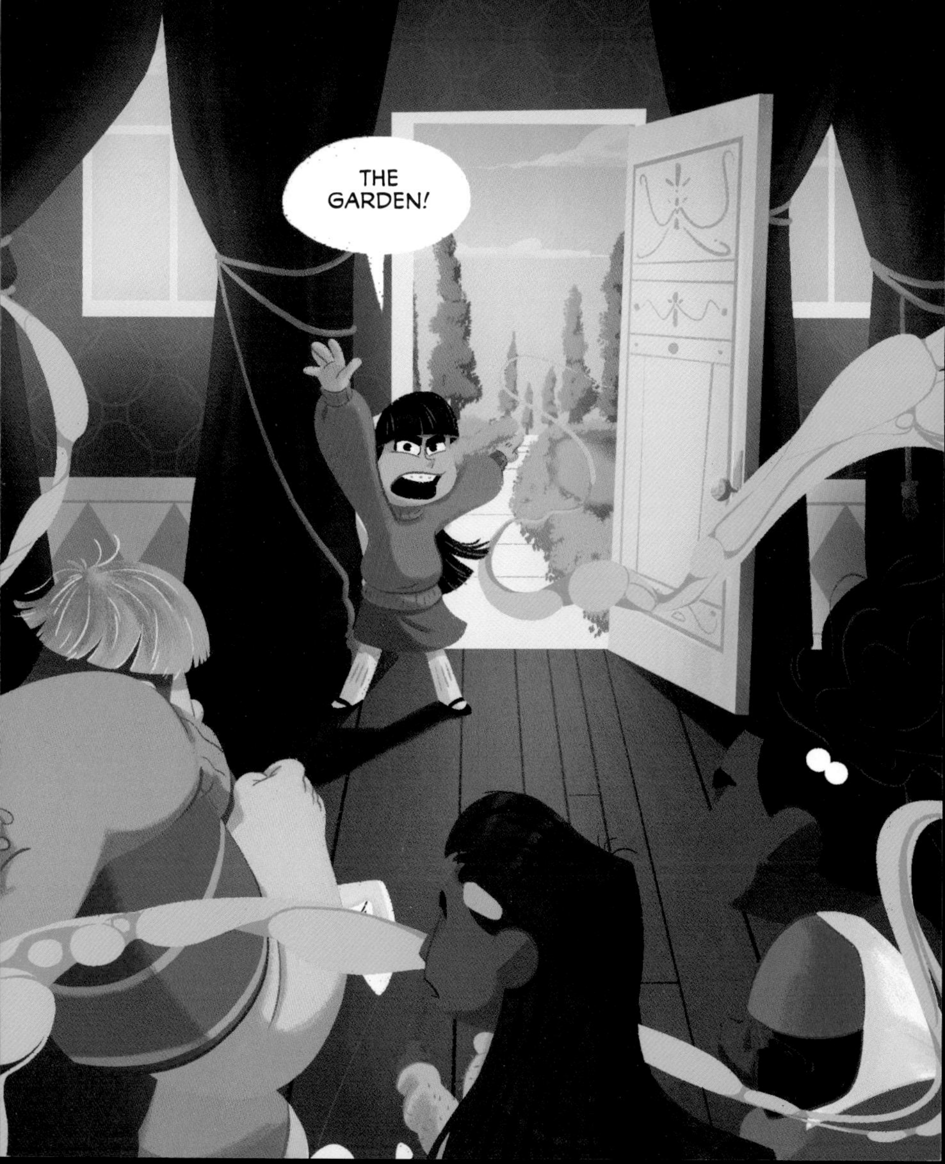
THE GARDEN!

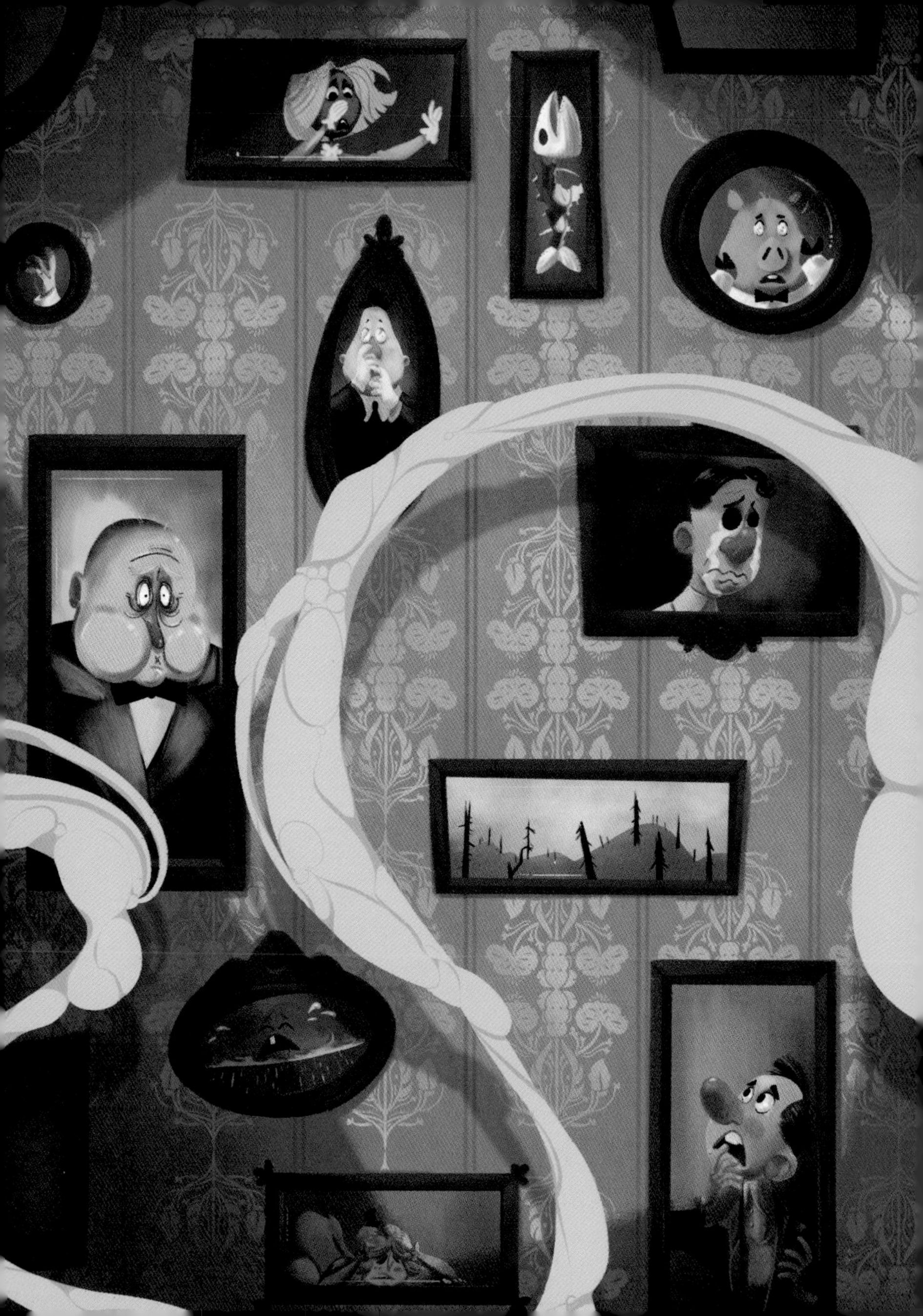

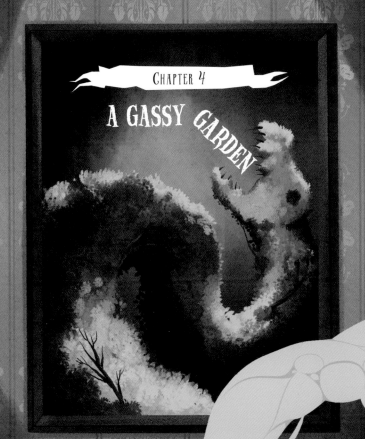

CHAPTER 4

A GASSY GARDEN

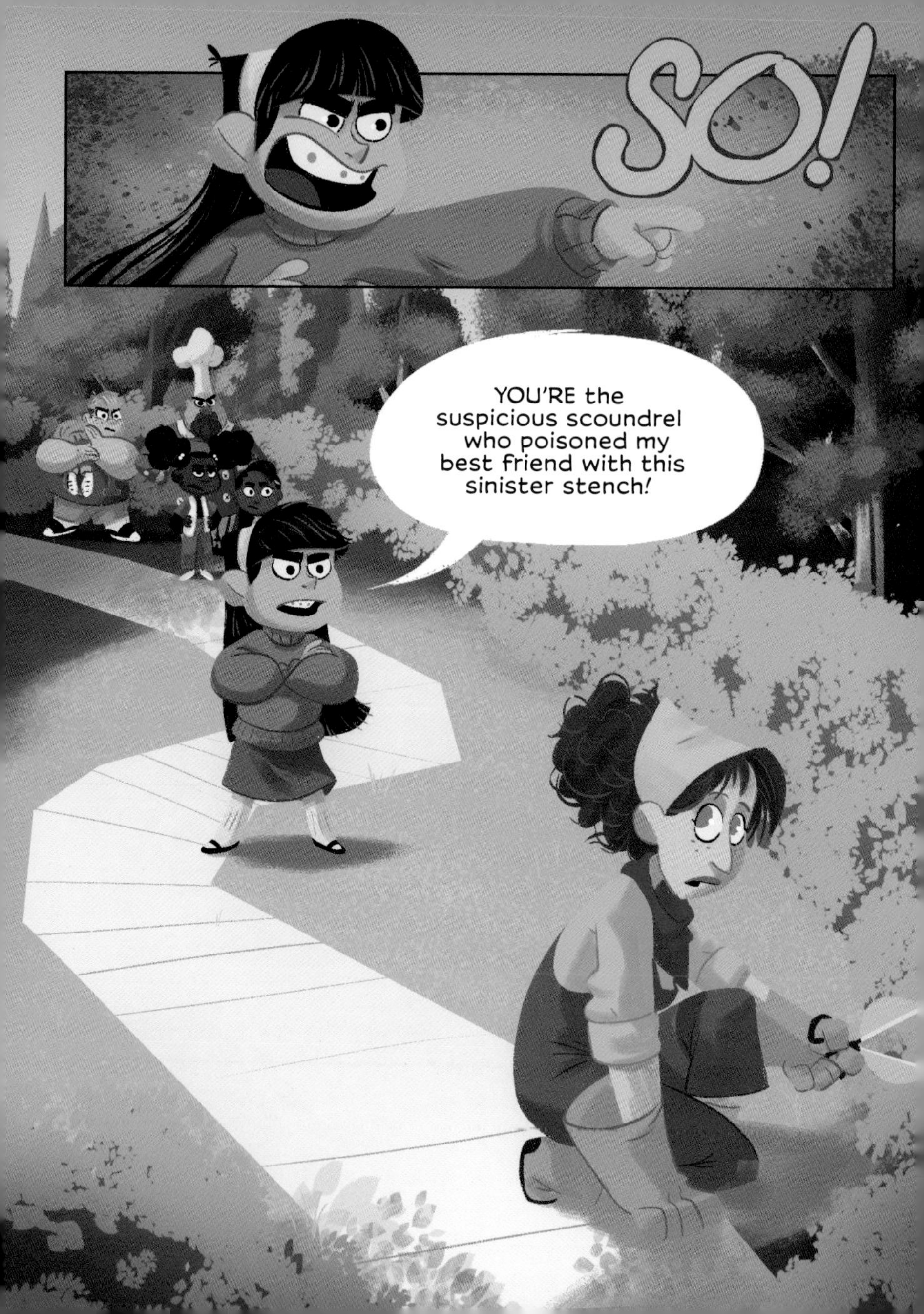
SO!
YOU'RE the suspicious scoundrel who poisoned my best friend with this sinister stench!

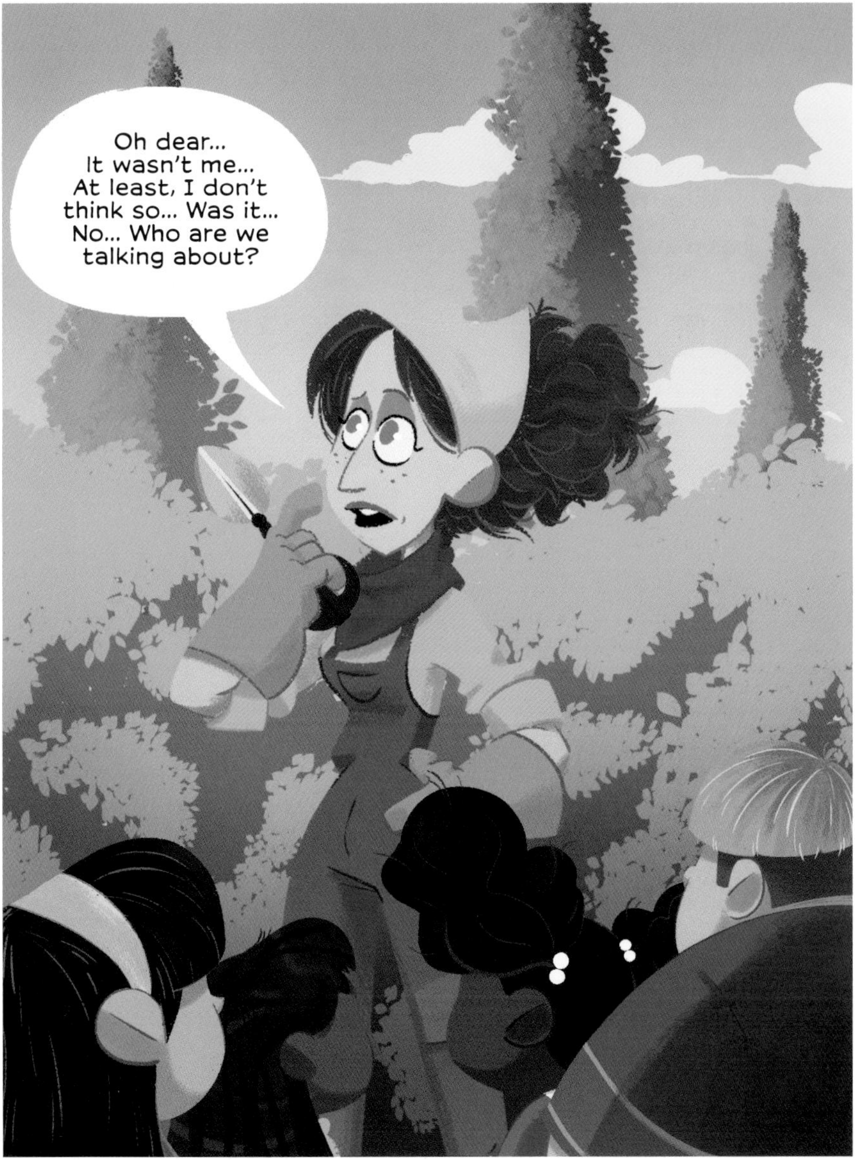
Oh dear...
It wasn't me...
At least, I don't
think so... Was it...
No... Who are we
talking about?

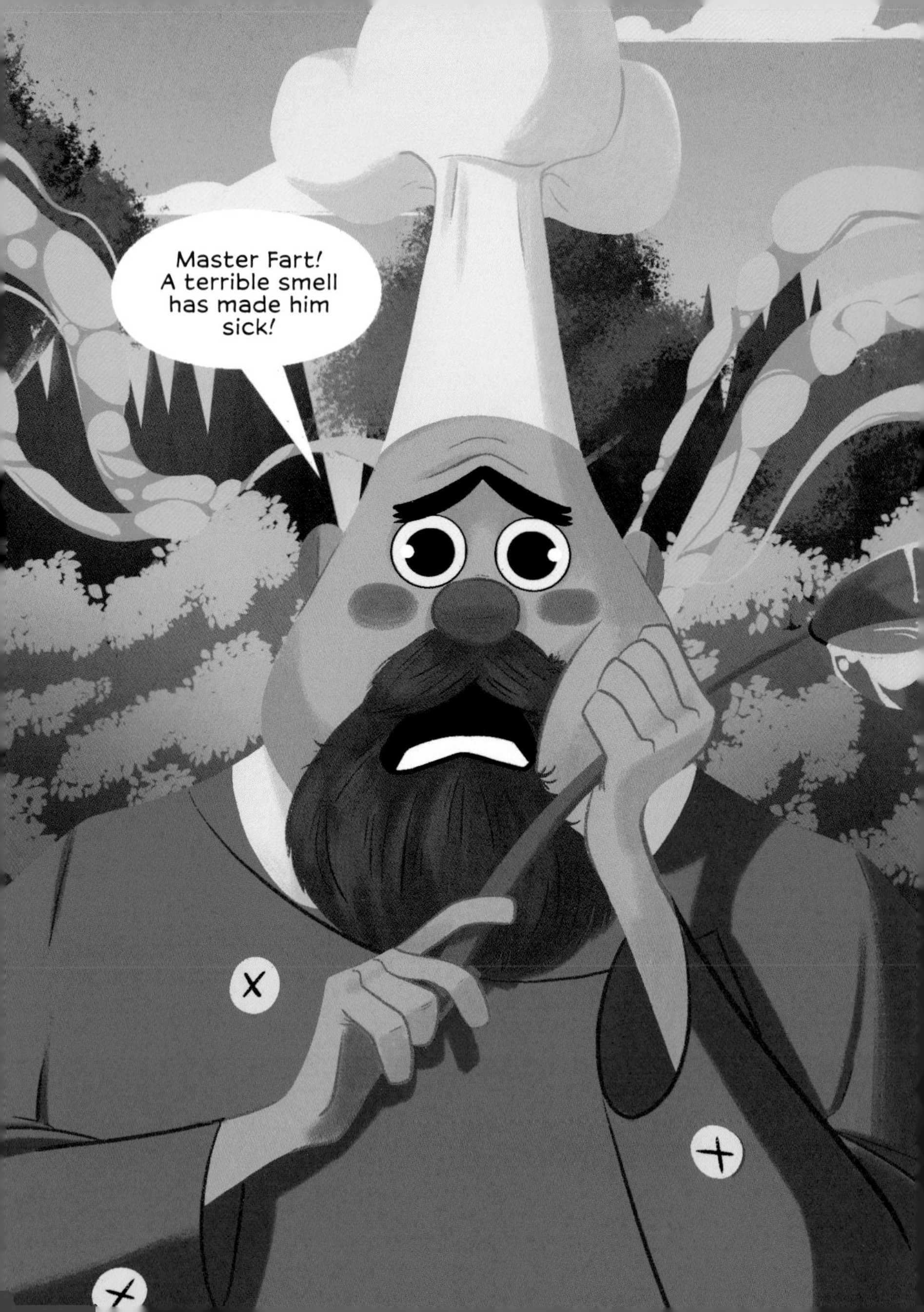
Master Fart! A terrible smell has made him sick!

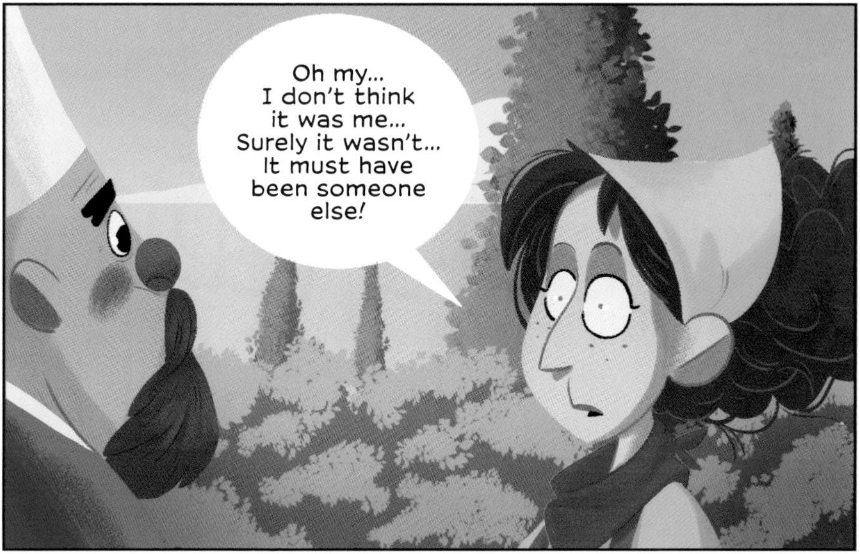
Oh my... I don't think it was me... Surely it wasn't... It must have been someone else!

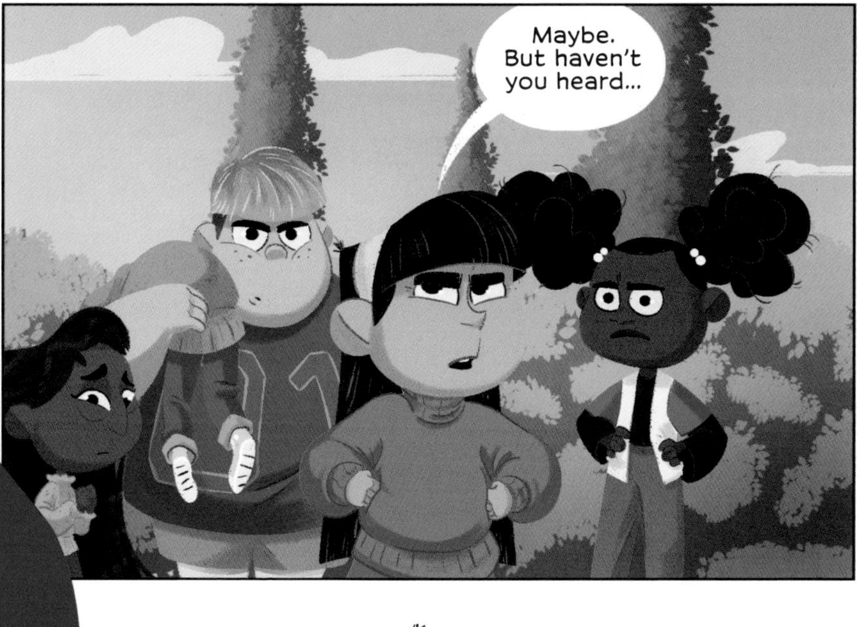
Maybe. But haven't you heard...

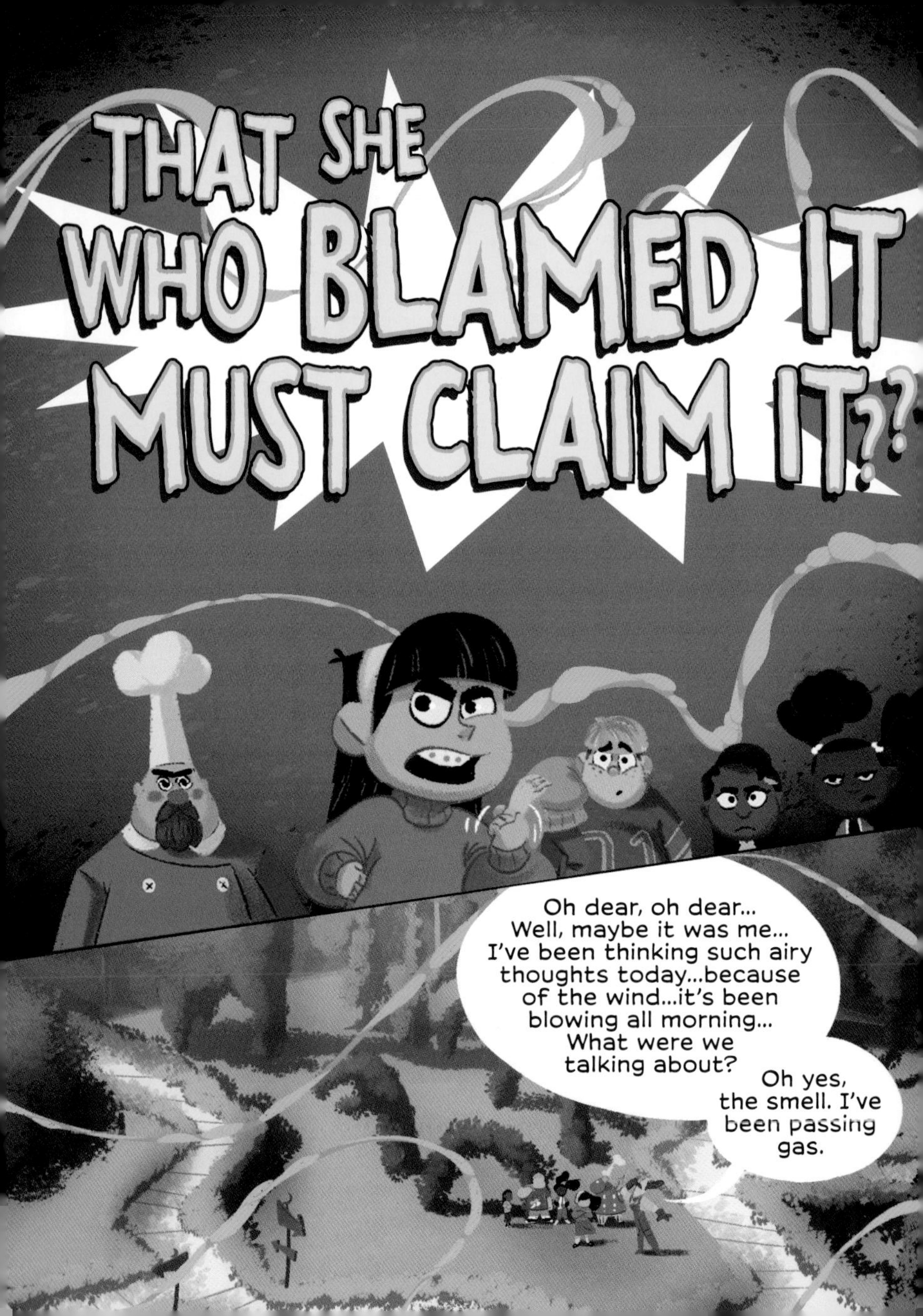
THAT SHE WHO BLAMED IT MUST CLAIM IT?!
Oh dear, oh dear... Well, maybe it was me... I've been thinking such airy thoughts today...because of the wind...it's been blowing all morning... What were we talking about?
Oh yes, the smell. I've been passing gas.

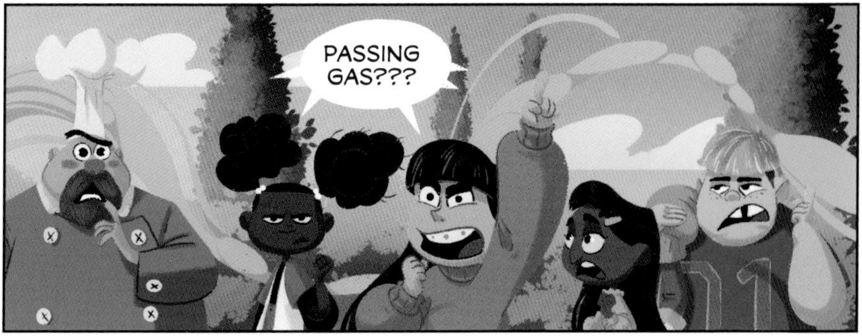
PASSING GAS???

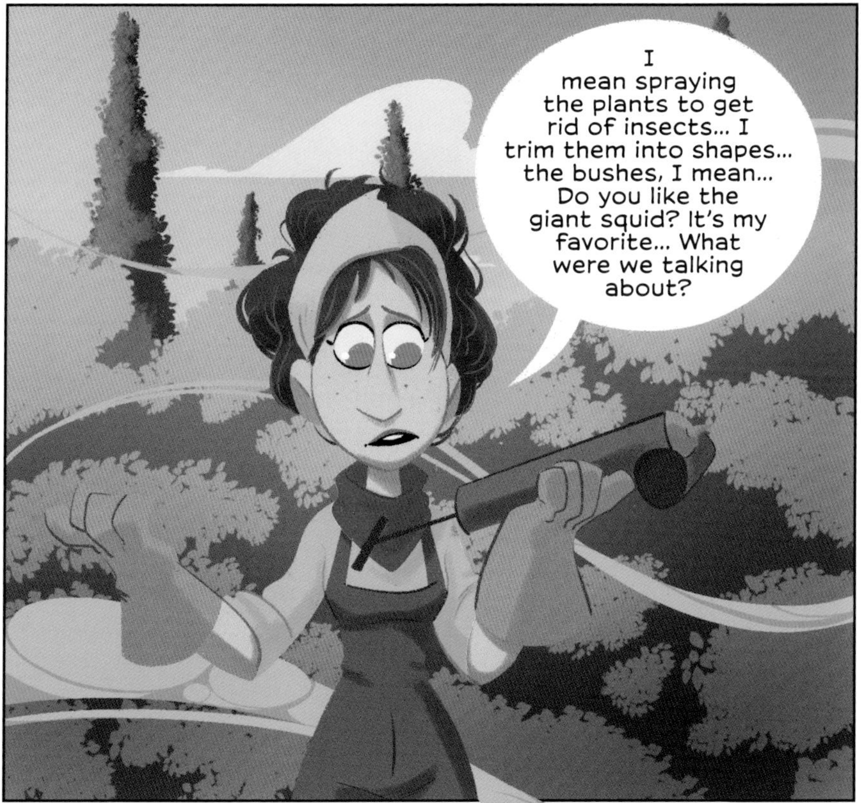
I mean spraying the plants to get rid of insects... I trim them into shapes... the bushes, I mean... Do you like the giant squid? It's my favorite... What were we talking about?

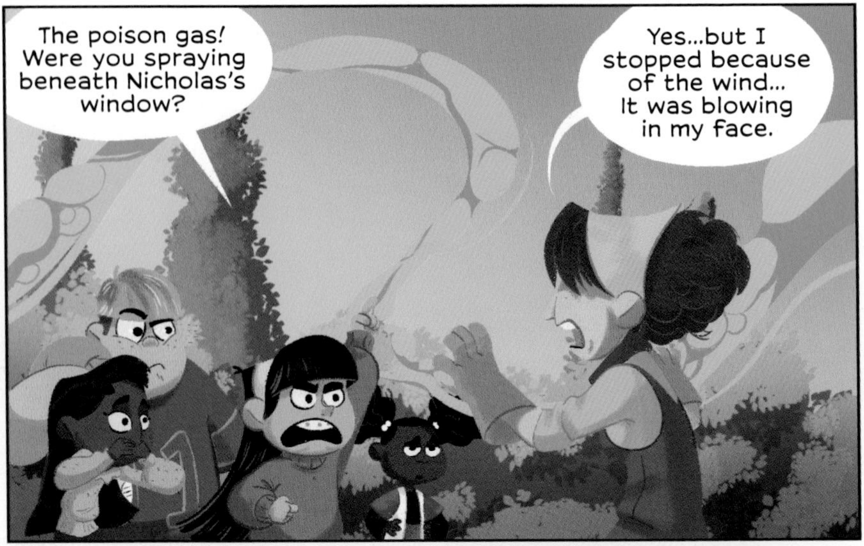
The poison gas! Were you spraying beneath Nicholas's window?
Yes...but I stopped because of the wind... It was blowing in my face.

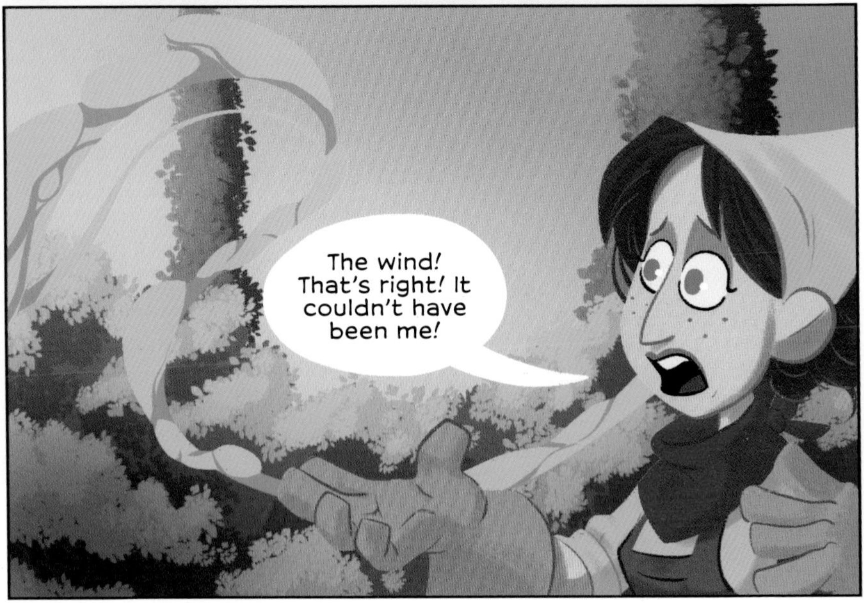
The wind! That's right! It couldn't have been me!

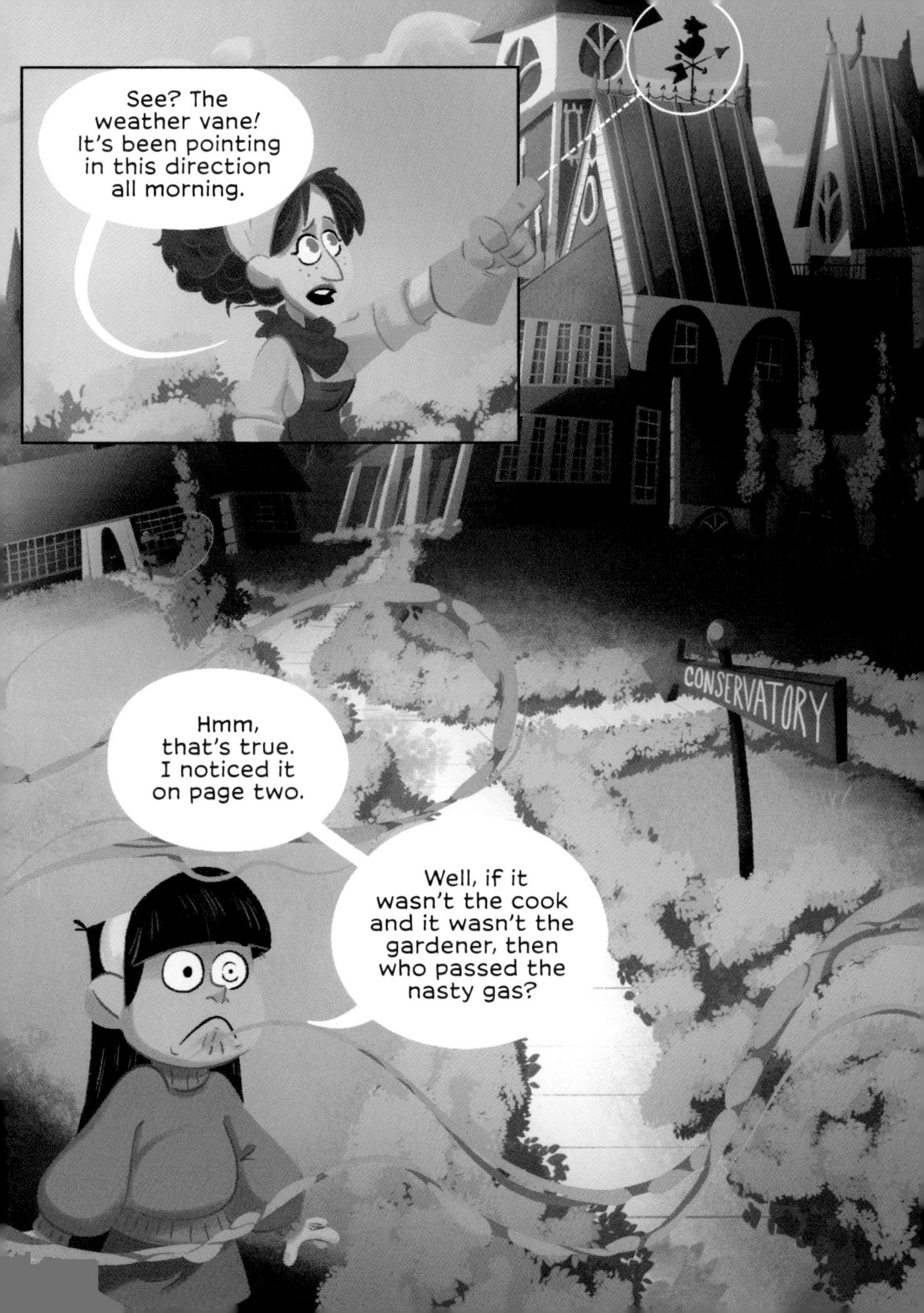
See? The weather vane! It's been pointing in this direction all morning.
CONSERVATORY
Hmm, that's true. I noticed it on page two.
Well, if it wasn't the cook and it wasn't the gardener, then who passed the nasty gas?

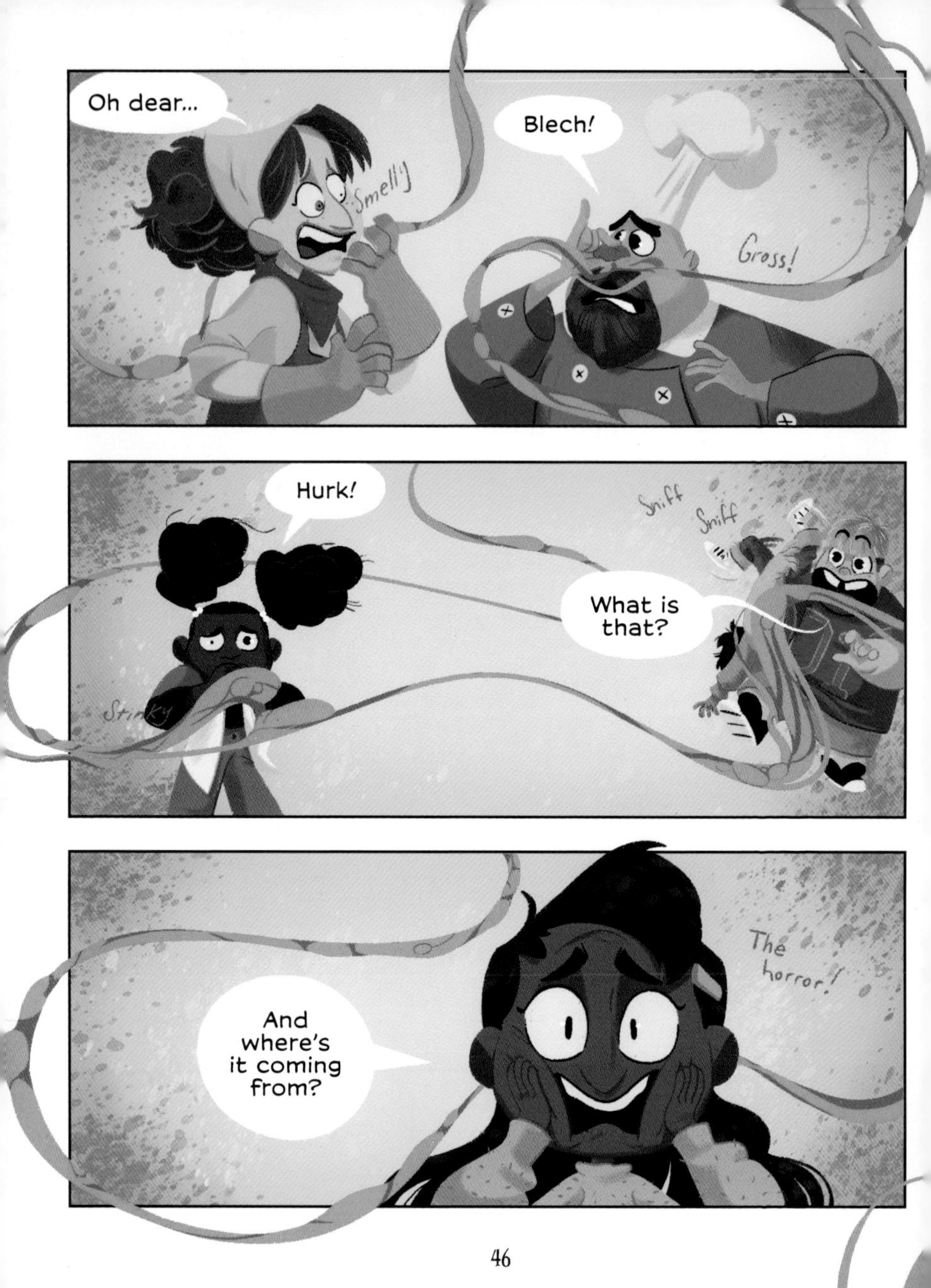
Oh dear...
Smelly
Blech!
Gross!
Hurk!
Sniff
Sniff
What is that?
Stinky
The horror!
And where's it coming from?

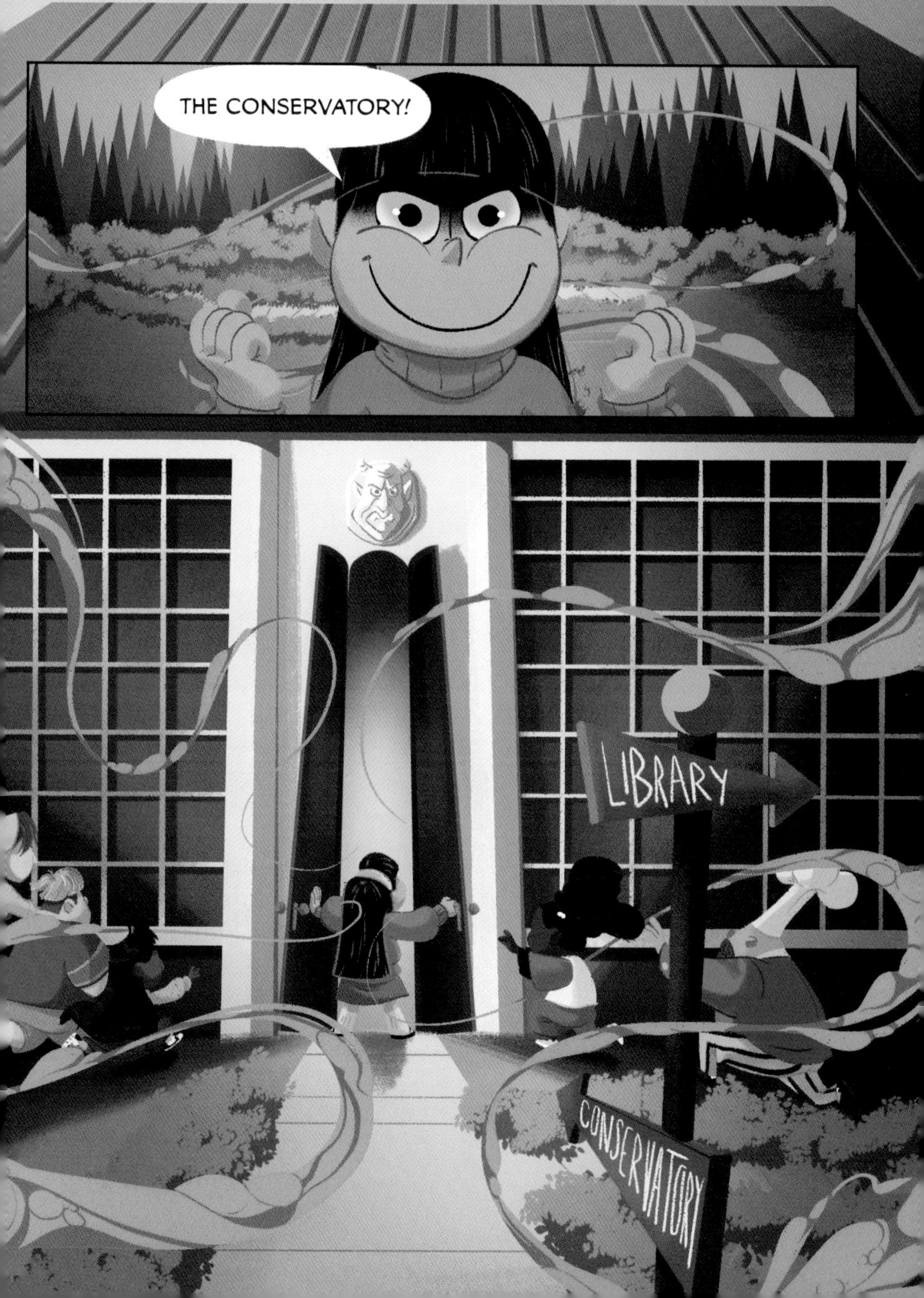
THE CONSERVATORY!
LIBRARY
CONSERVATORY

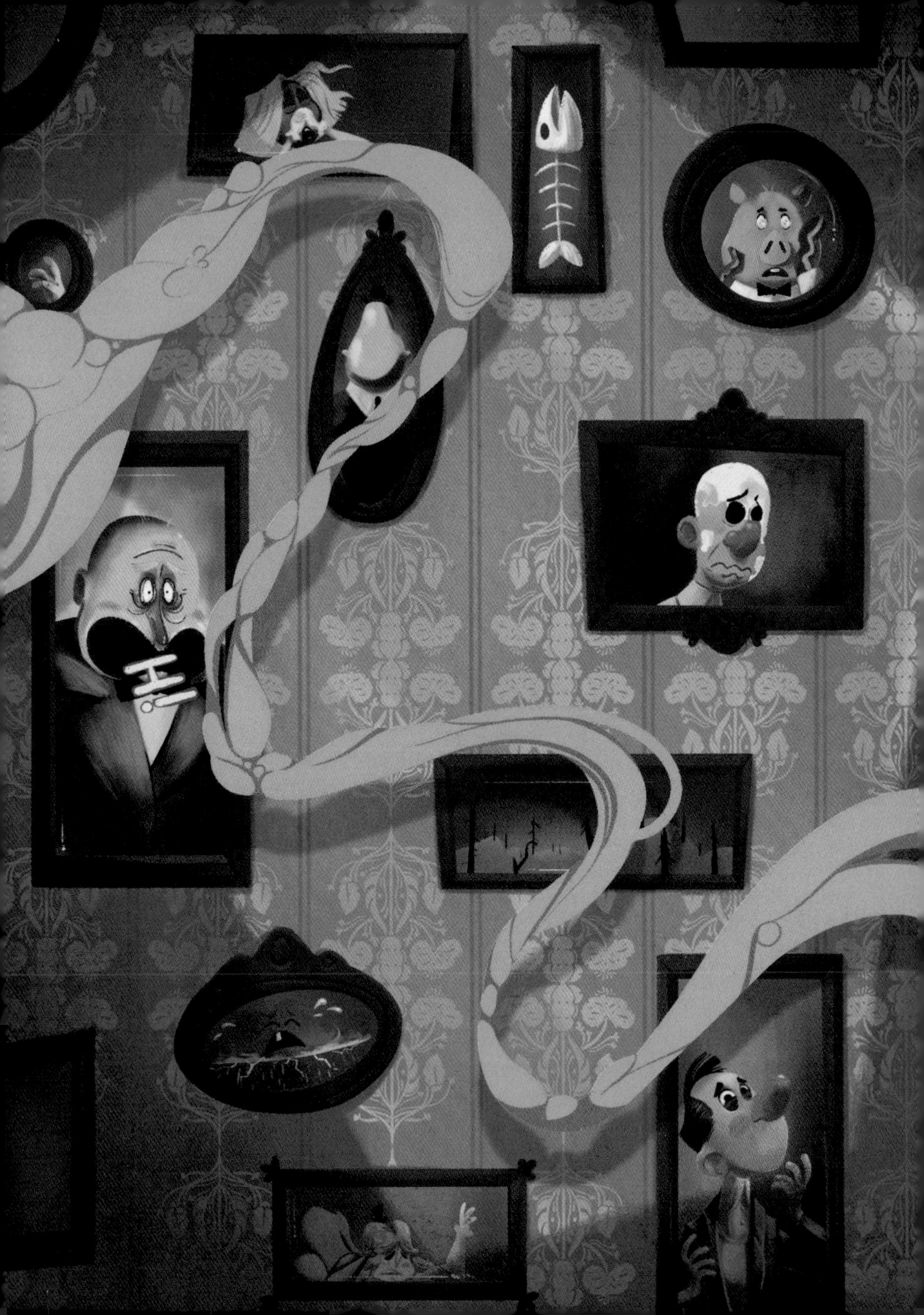

Chapter 5

The Tooting Tutor

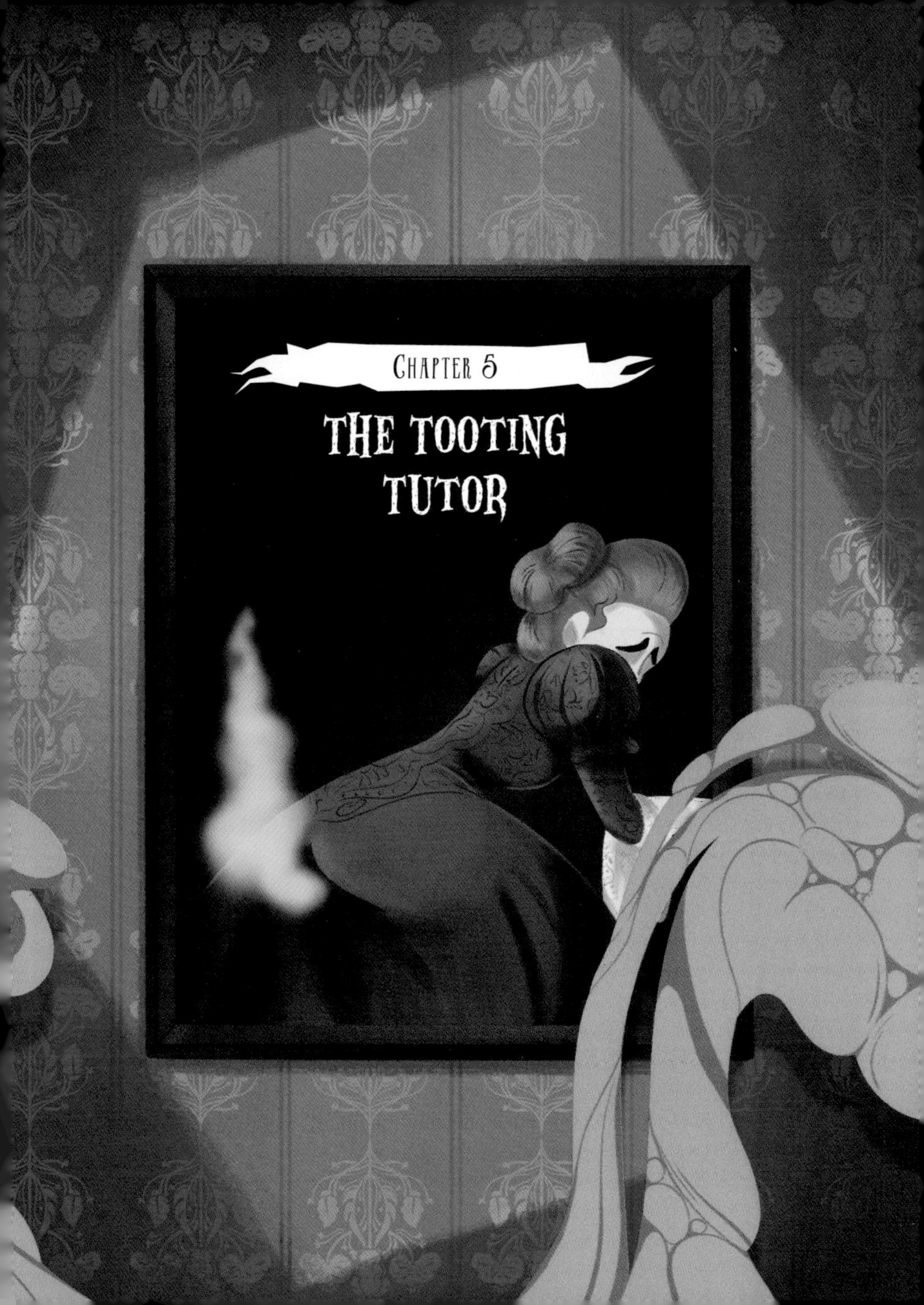

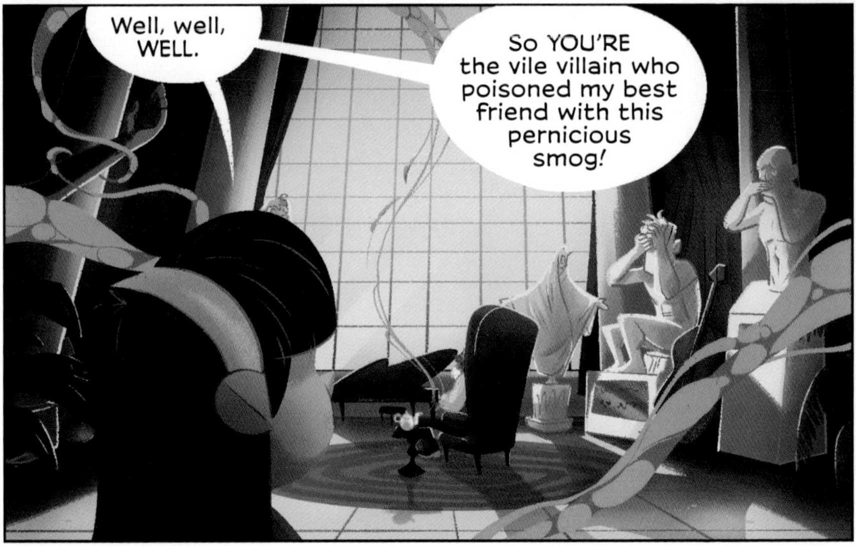
Well, well, WELL.
So YOU'RE the vile villain who poisoned my best friend with this pernicious smog!

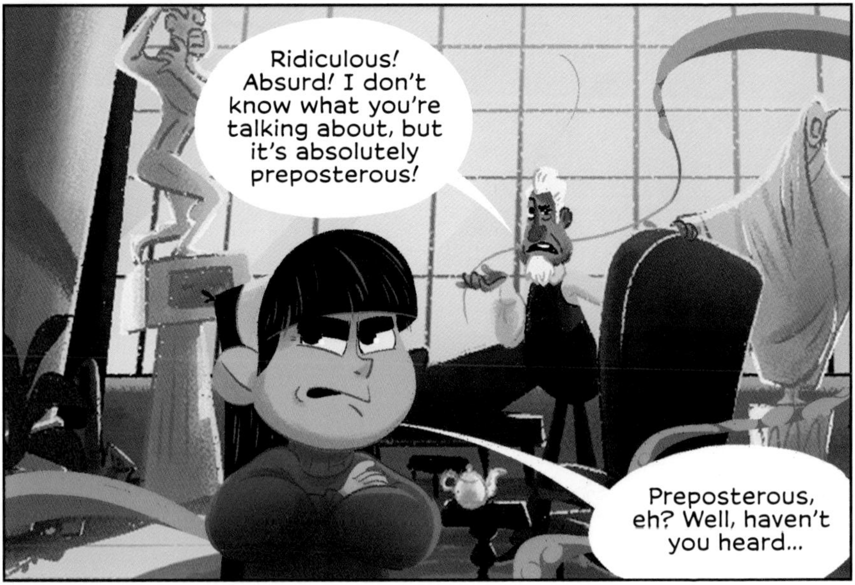
Ridiculous! Absurd! I don't know what you're talking about, but it's absolutely preposterous!
Preposterous, eh? Well, haven't you heard...

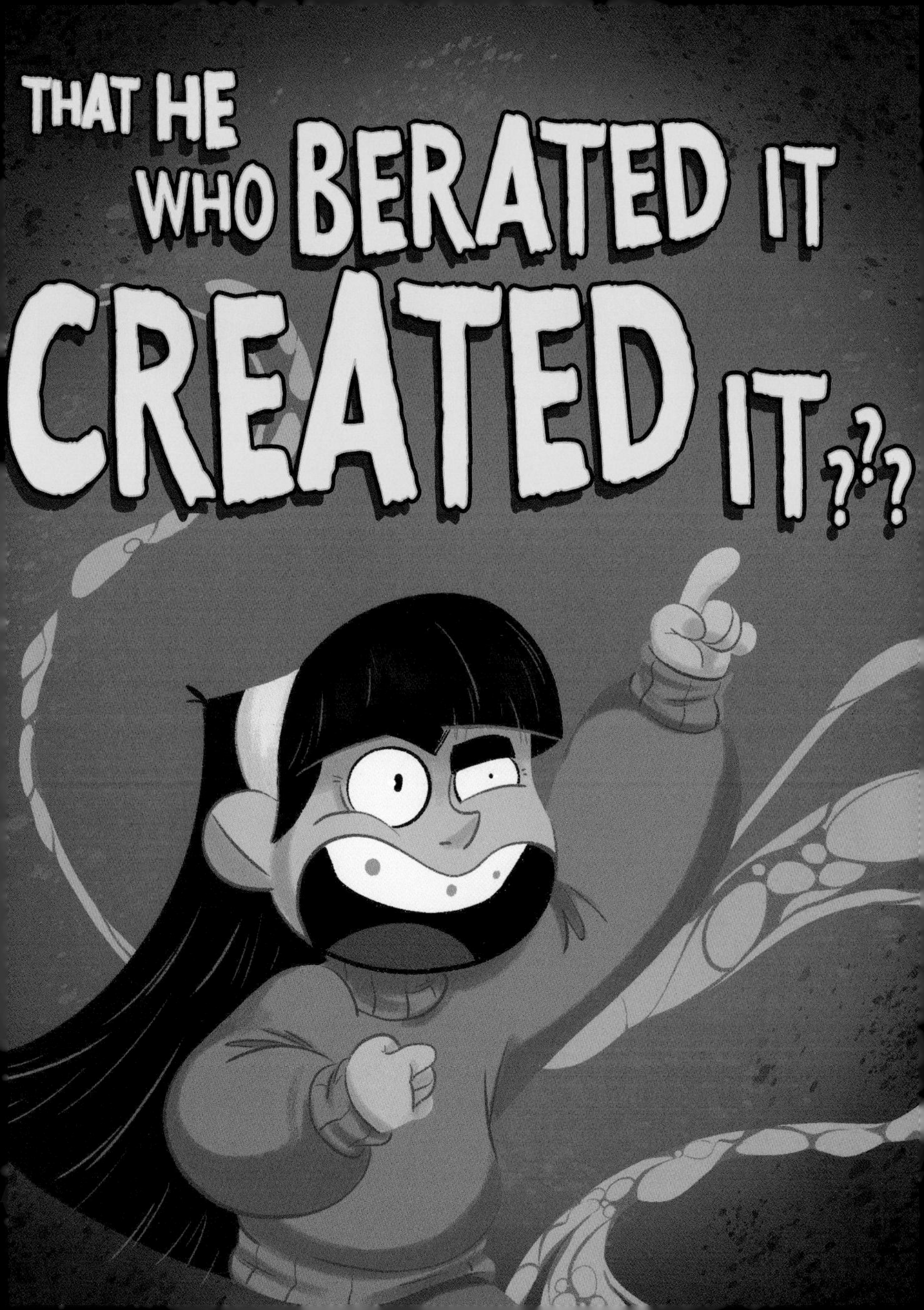
THAT HE WHO BERATED IT CREATED IT???

Indeed! I create many things. Symphonies! Sonatas! Waltzes! But none of them are rotten. In fact, they are beautiful.
Why, just now, I was tooting...
TOOTING?
Of course! On this magnificent trumpet.
Well, what's that smell, then?
My pu-erh tea.* For moistening the palate.

S. GLUM

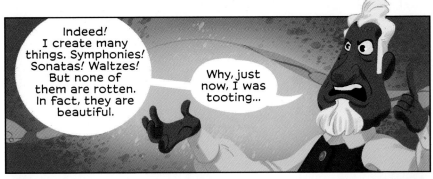

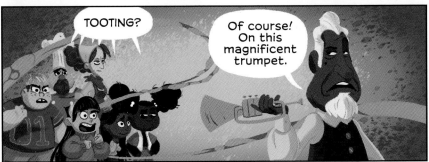

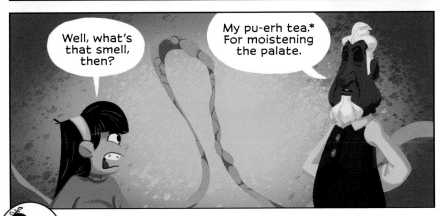

*PU-ERH TEA MAY BE PRONOUNCED "POO-ERH," BUT IT IS NOT MADE OF POO. IT IS A FERMENTED TEA FROM THE YUNNAN PROVINCE, AND A PERSONAL FAVORITE OF MINE. IT IS NOT FUNNY!

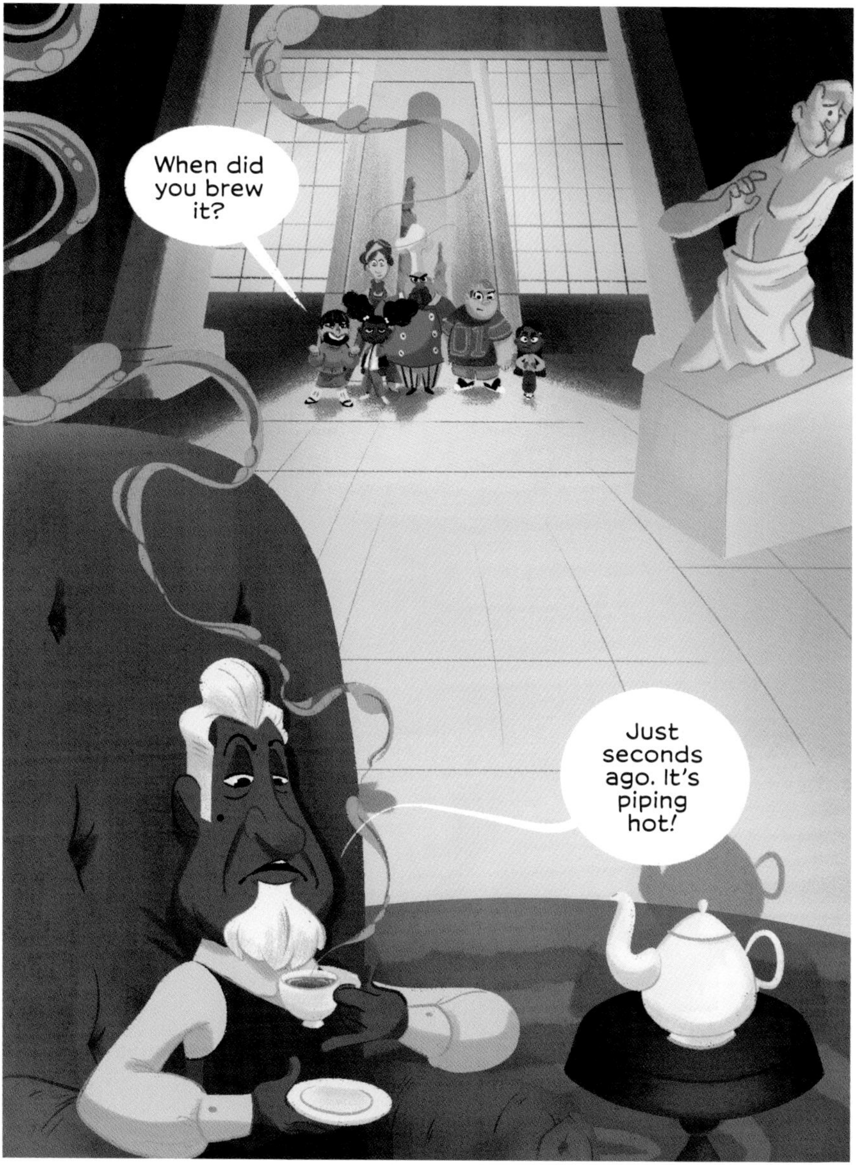
When did you brew it?
Just seconds ago. It's piping hot!

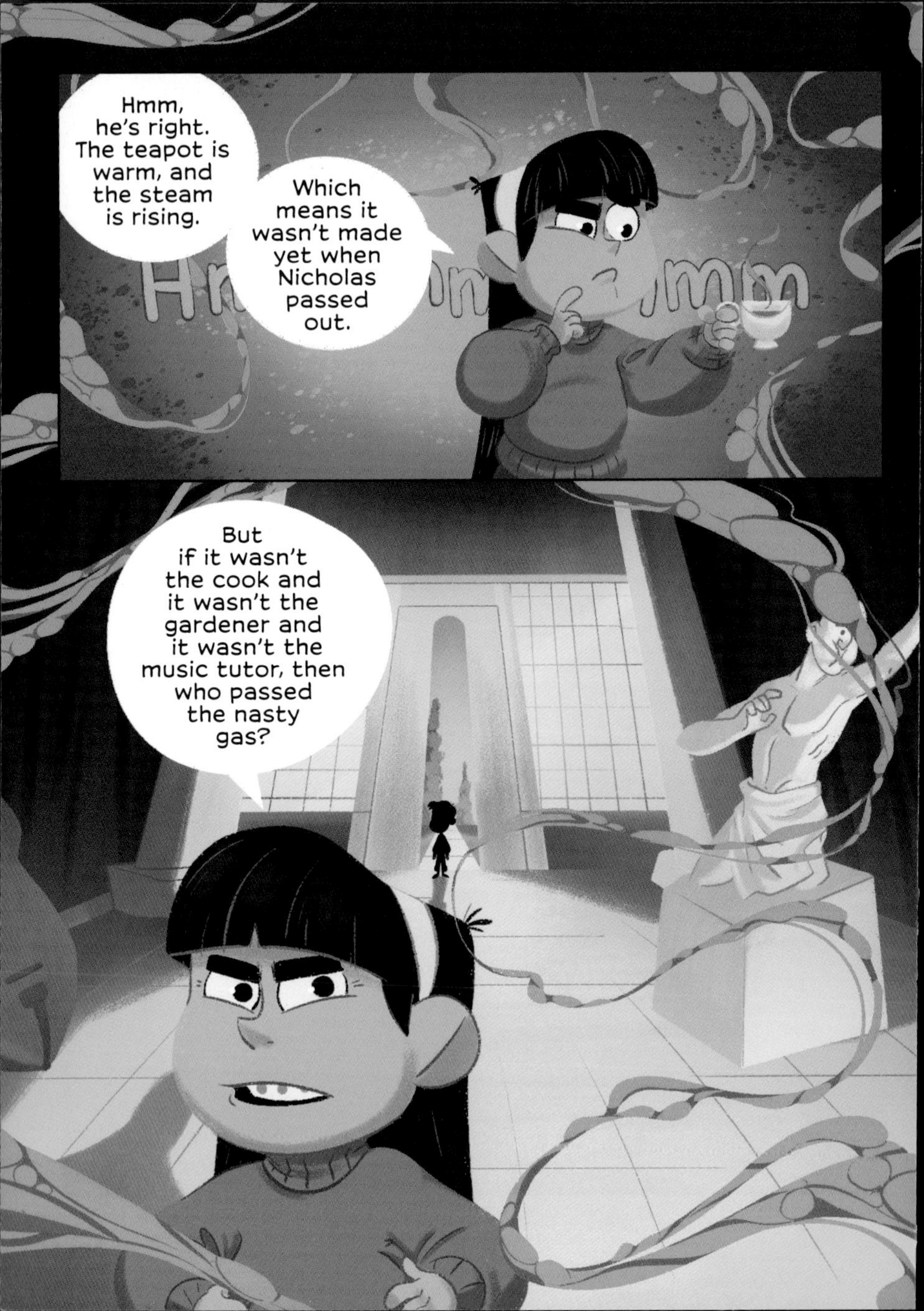
Hmm, he's right. The teapot is warm, and the steam is rising.
Which means it wasn't made yet when Nicholas passed out.
But if it wasn't the cook and it wasn't the gardener and it wasn't the music tutor, then who passed the nasty gas?

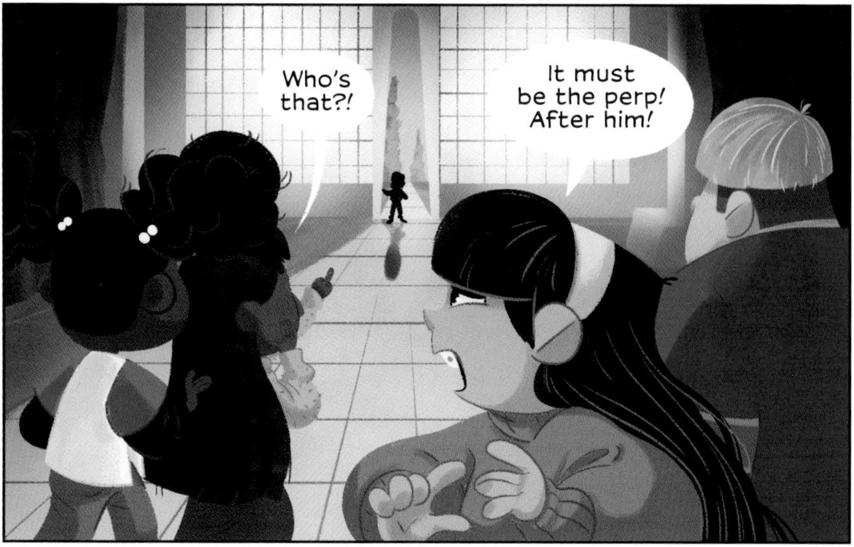
Who's that?!
It must be the perp! After him!

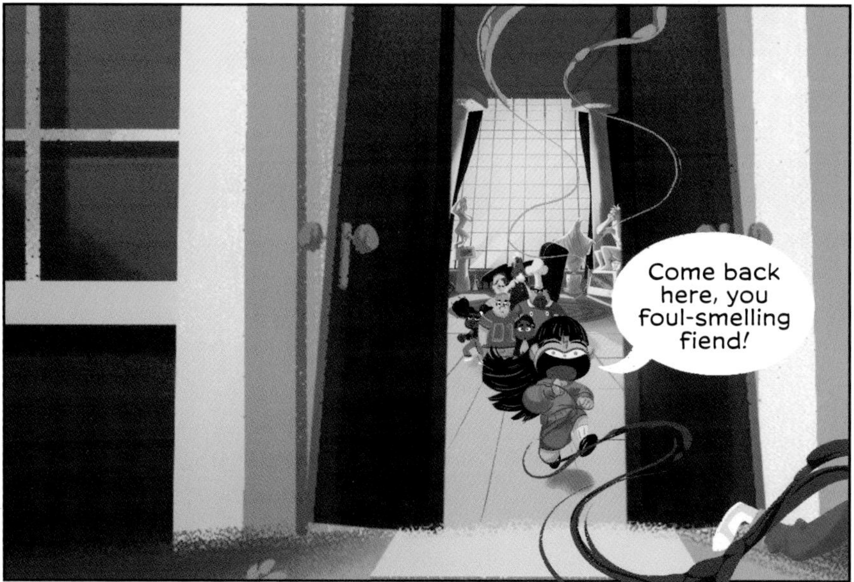
Come back here, you foul-smelling fiend!

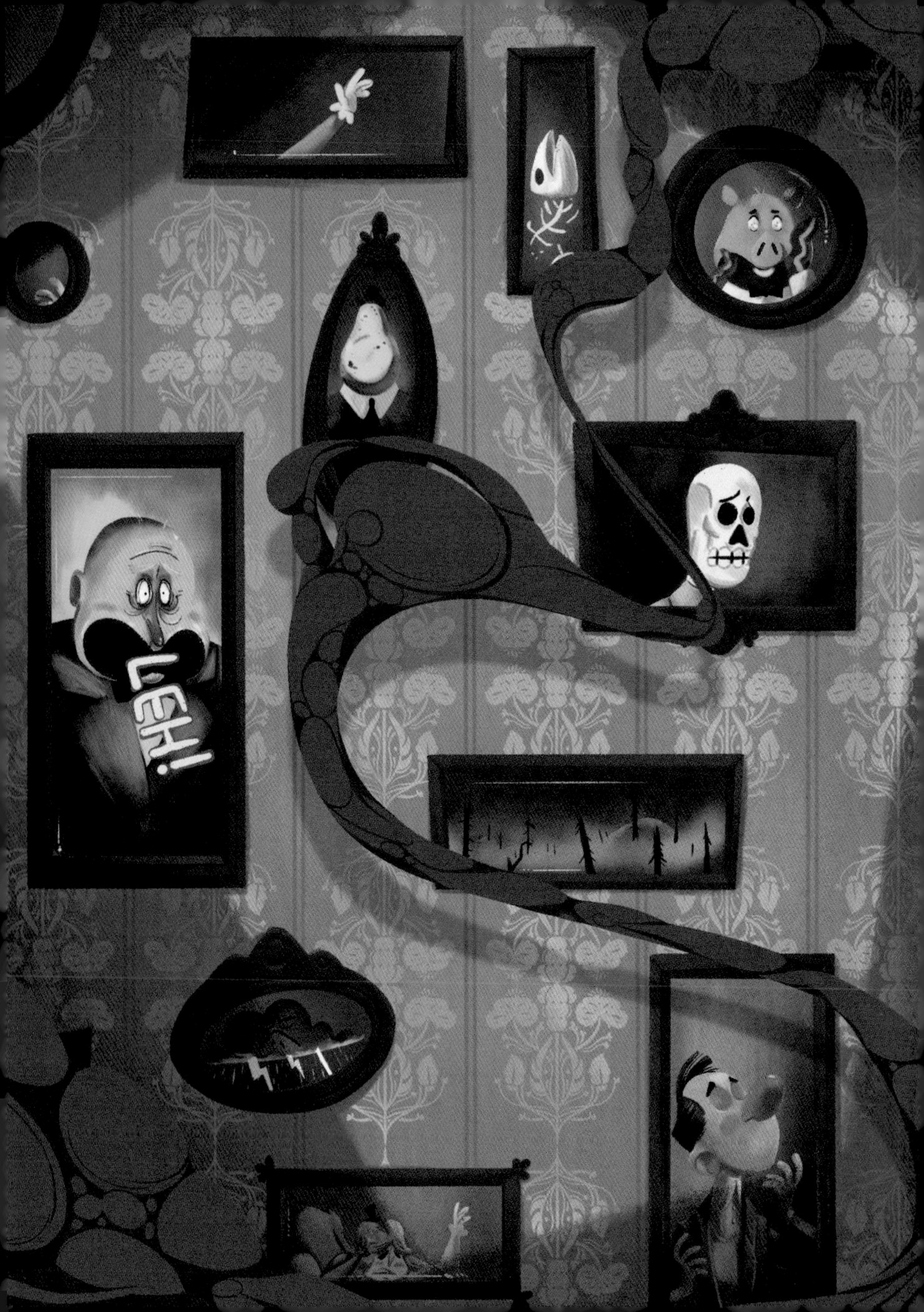
LEH!

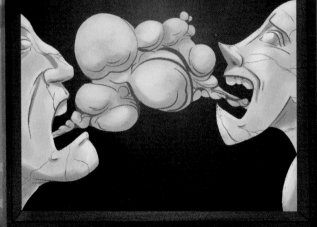

CHAPTER 6

MYSTERY (BURP) SOLVED!

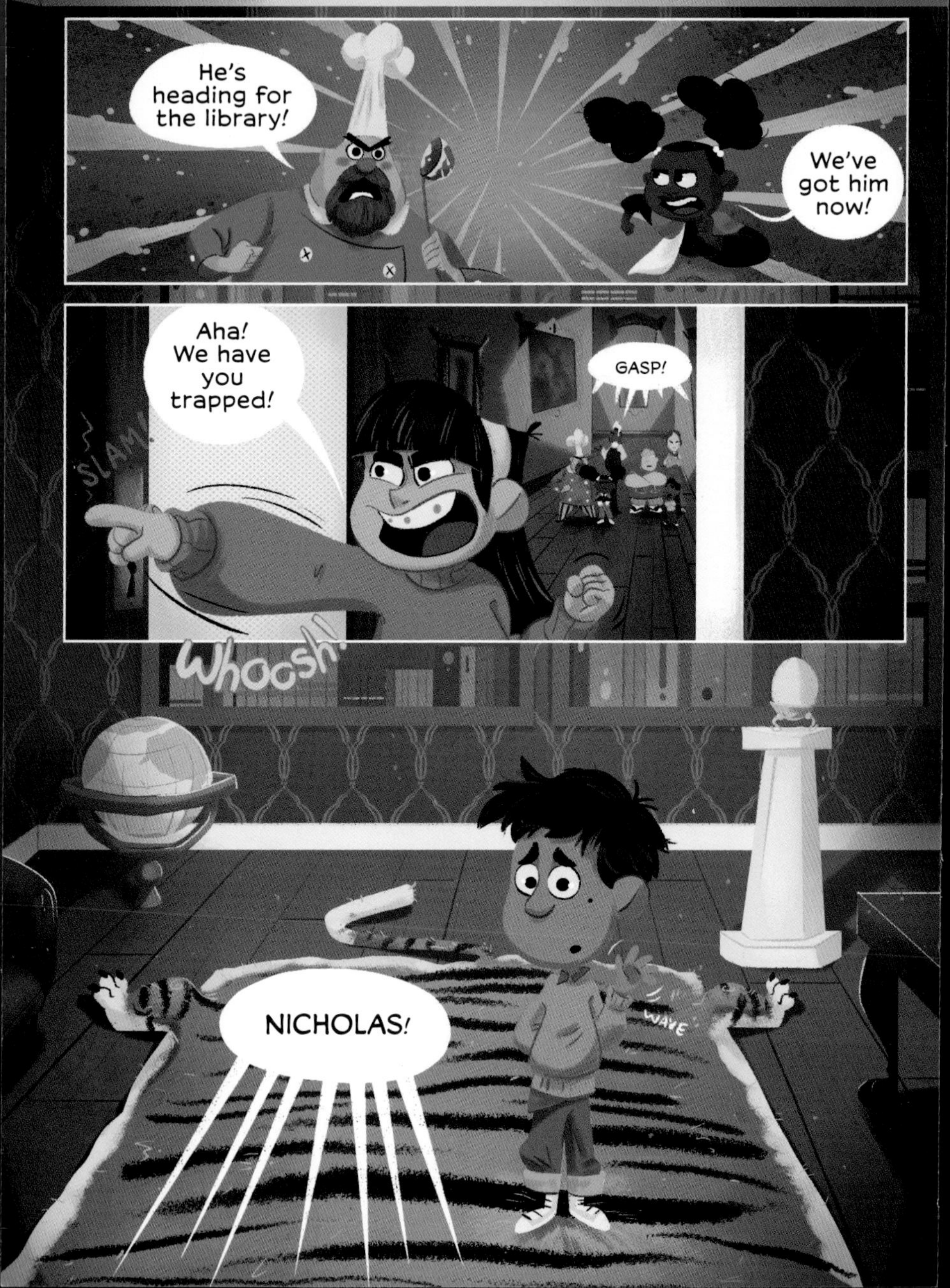
He's heading for the library!
We've got him now!
Aha! We have you trapped!
SLAM!
GASP!
Whoosh!
NICHOLAS!
WAVE

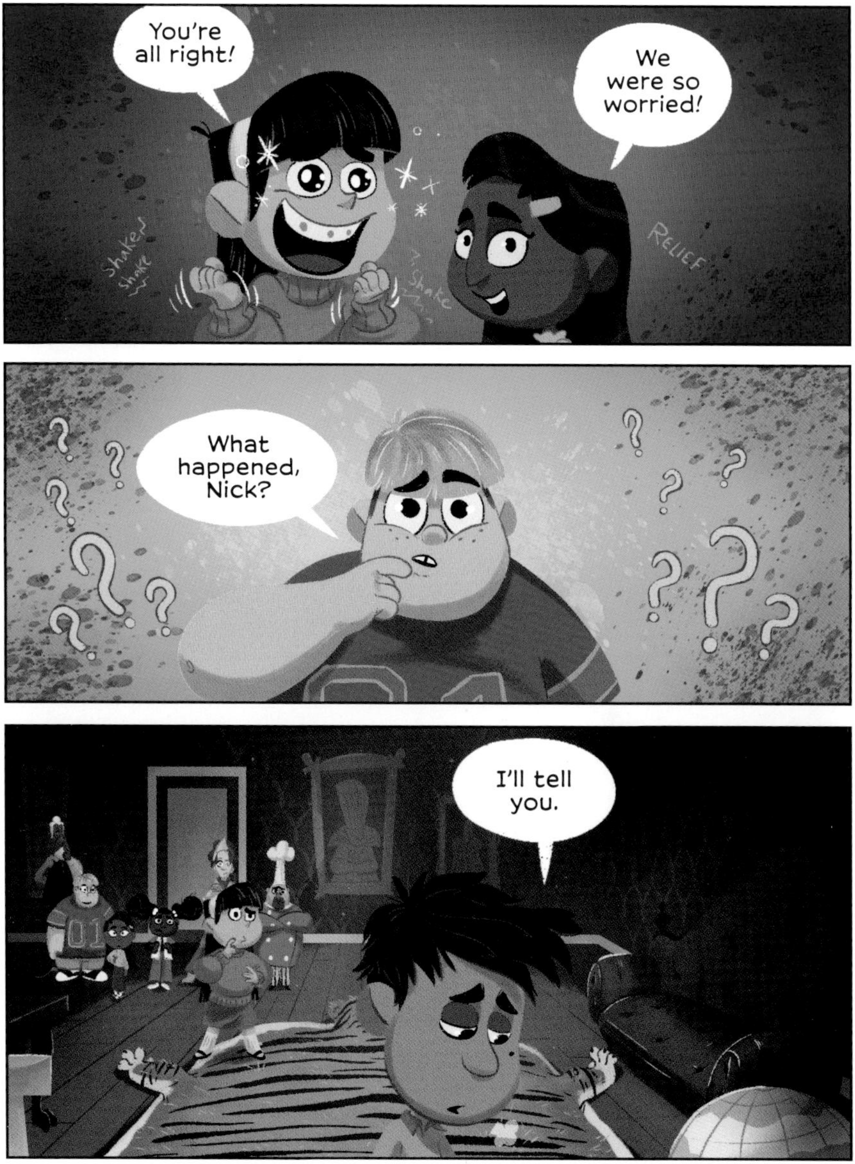
You're all right!
We were so worried!
Shake
Shake
Shake
RELIEF
What happened, Nick?
I'll tell you.

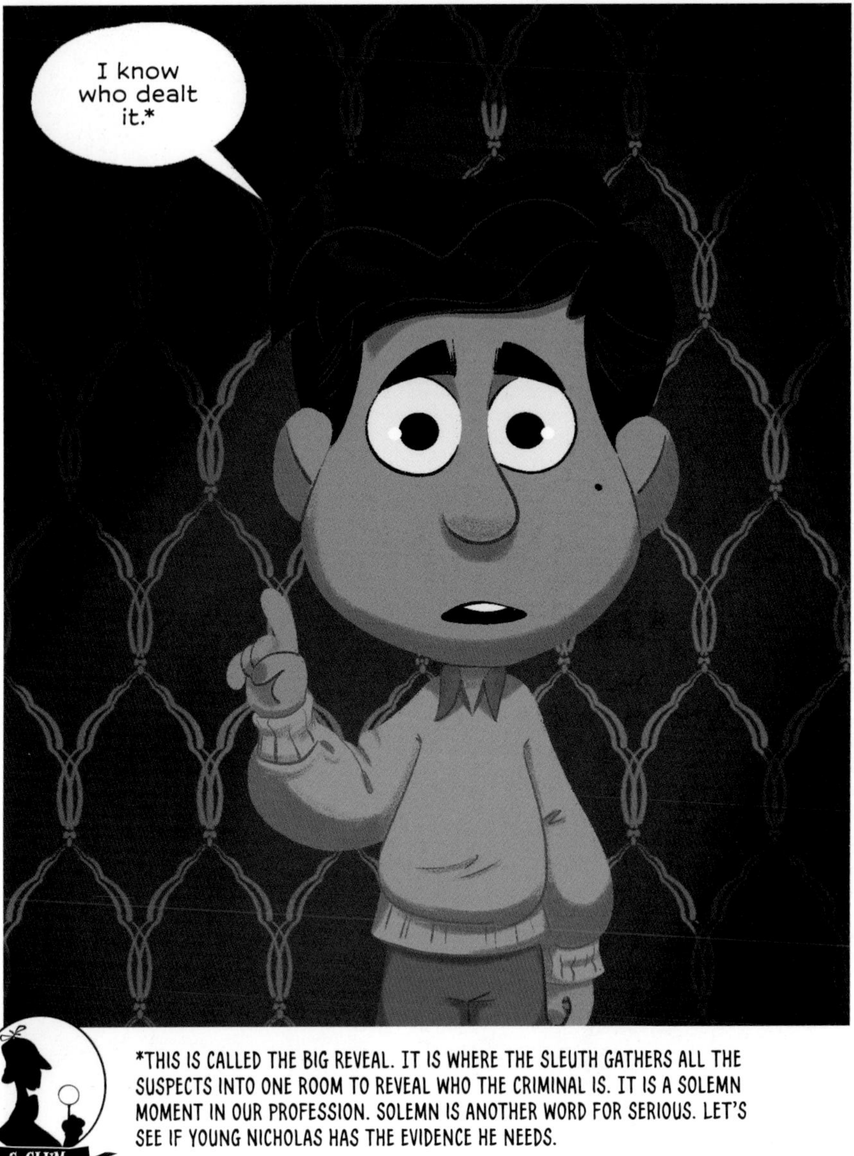
I know who dealt it.*

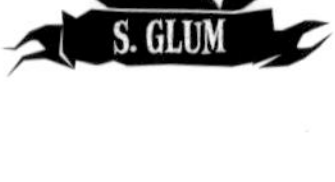
S. GLUM

*THIS IS CALLED THE BIG REVEAL. IT IS WHERE THE SLEUTH GATHERS ALL THE SUSPECTS INTO ONE ROOM TO REVEAL WHO THE CRIMINAL IS. IT IS A SOLEMN MOMENT IN OUR PROFESSION. SOLEMN IS ANOTHER WORD FOR SERIOUS. LET'S SEE IF YOUNG NICHOLAS HAS THE EVIDENCE HE NEEDS.

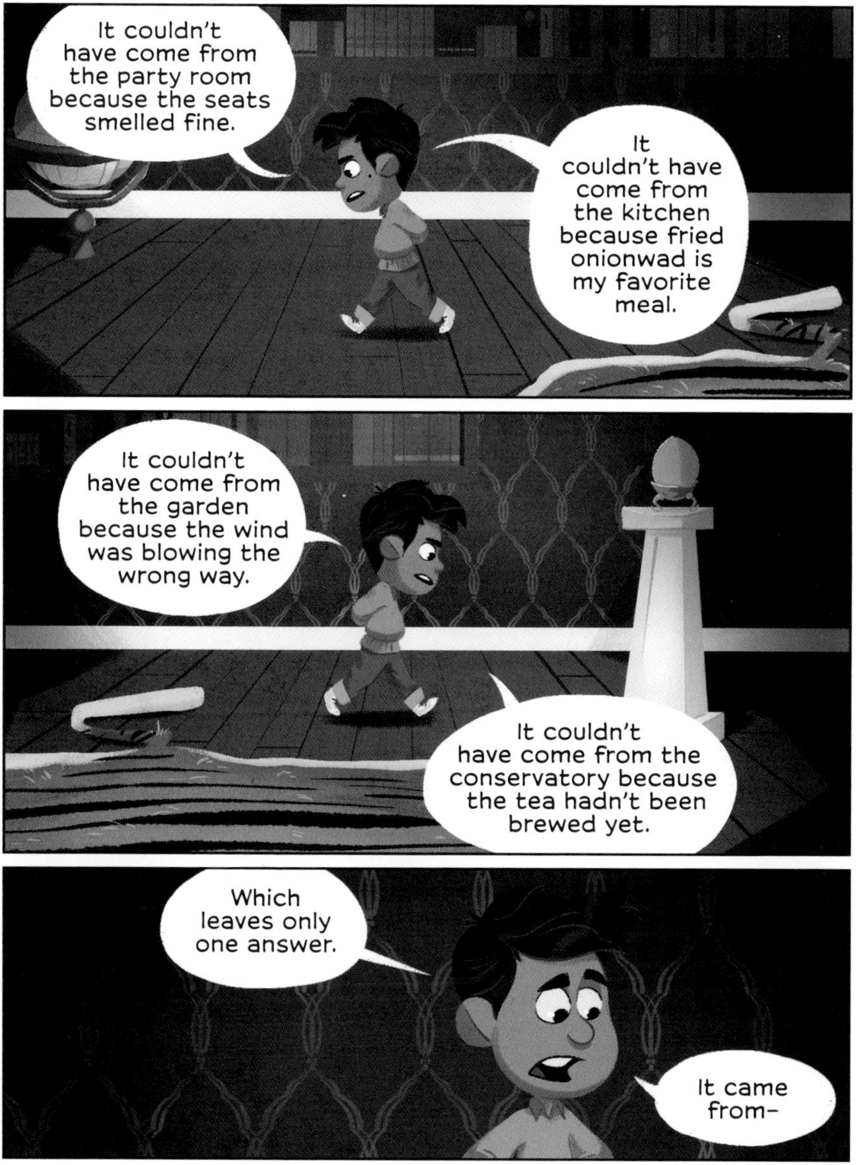

It couldn't have come from the party room because the seats smelled fine.
It couldn't have come from the kitchen because fried onionwad is my favorite meal.
It couldn't have come from the garden because the wind was blowing the wrong way.
It couldn't have come from the conservatory because the tea hadn't been brewed yet.
Which leaves only one answer.
It came from–

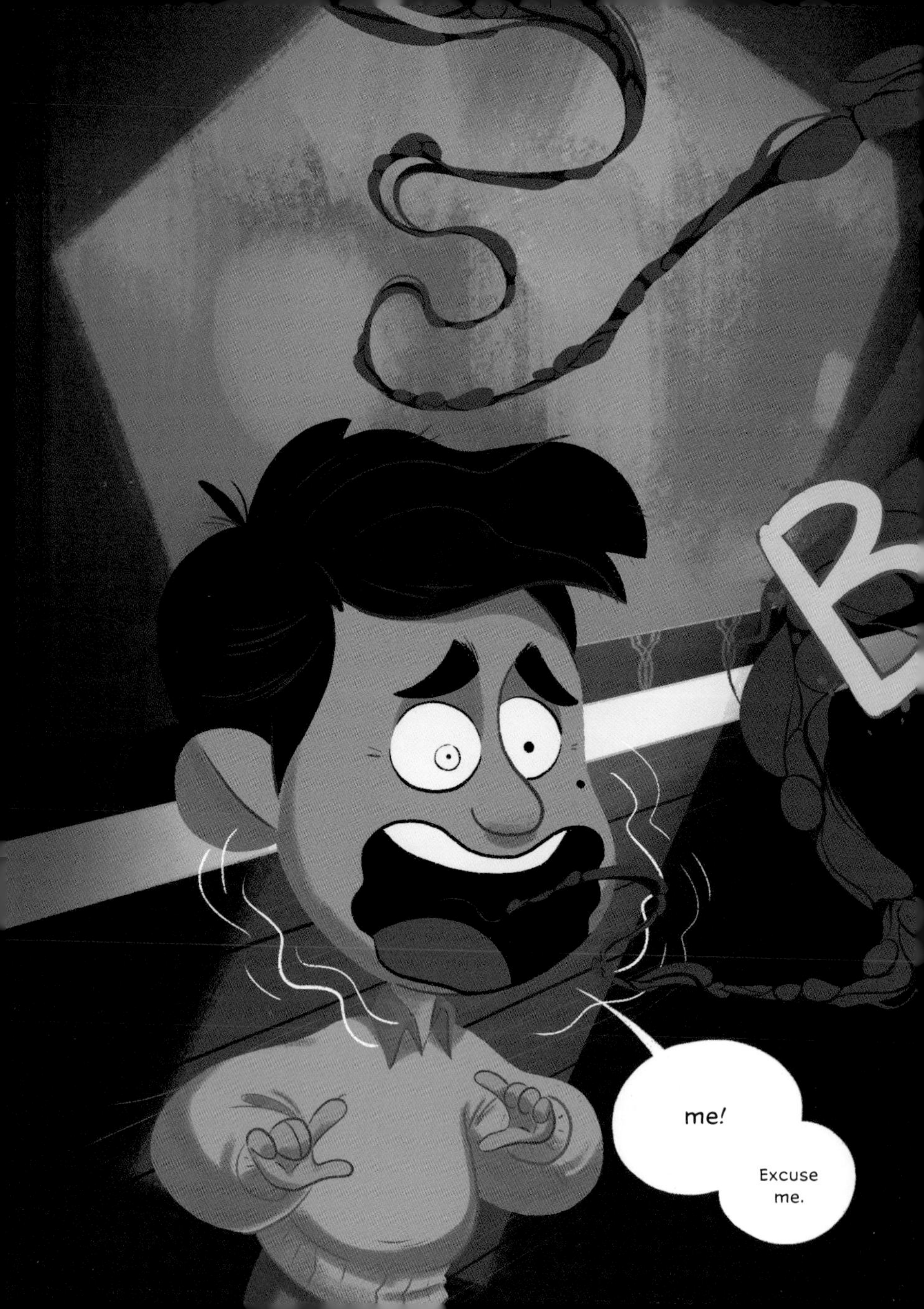
me!
Excuse me.

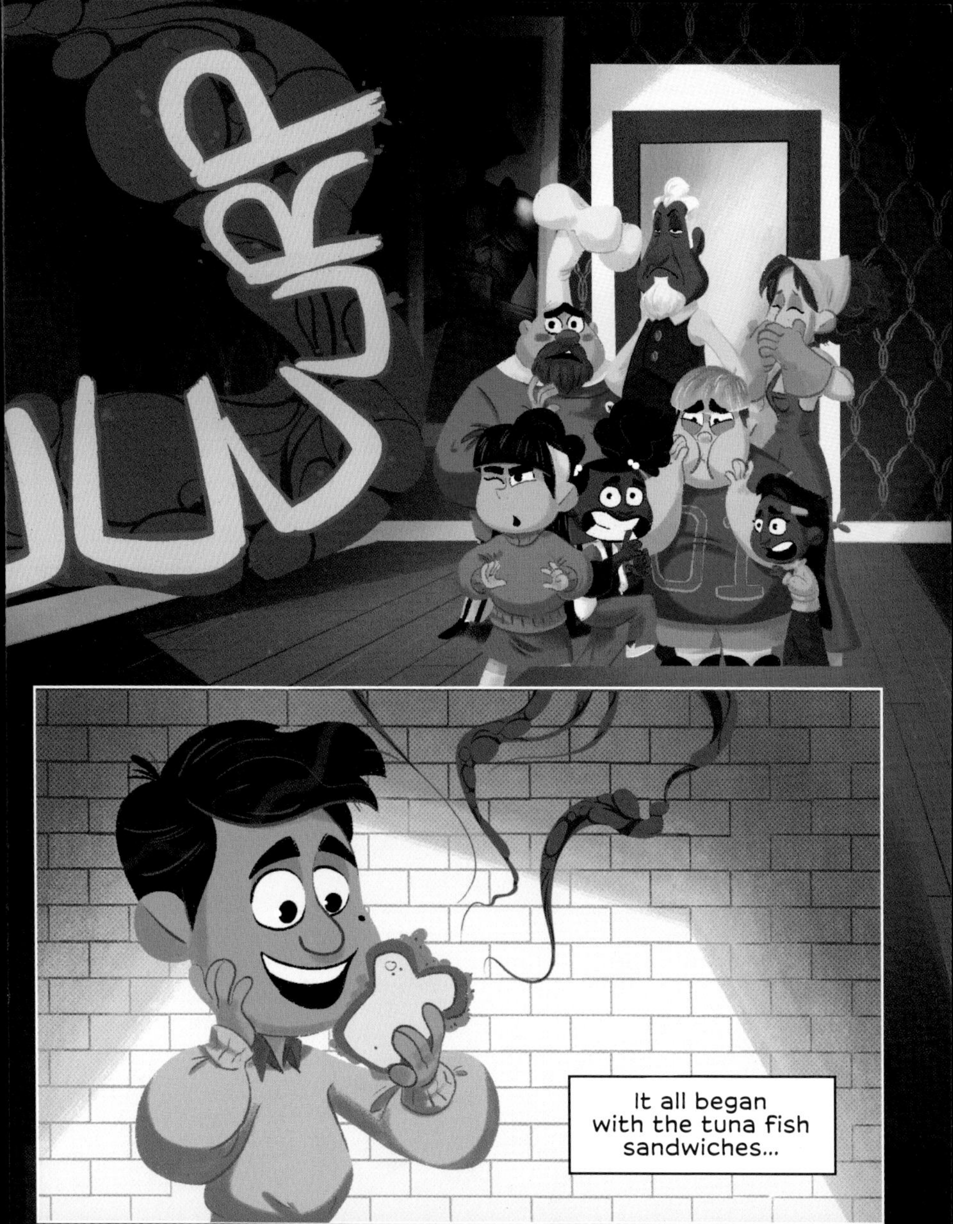
It all began
with the tuna fish
sandwiches...

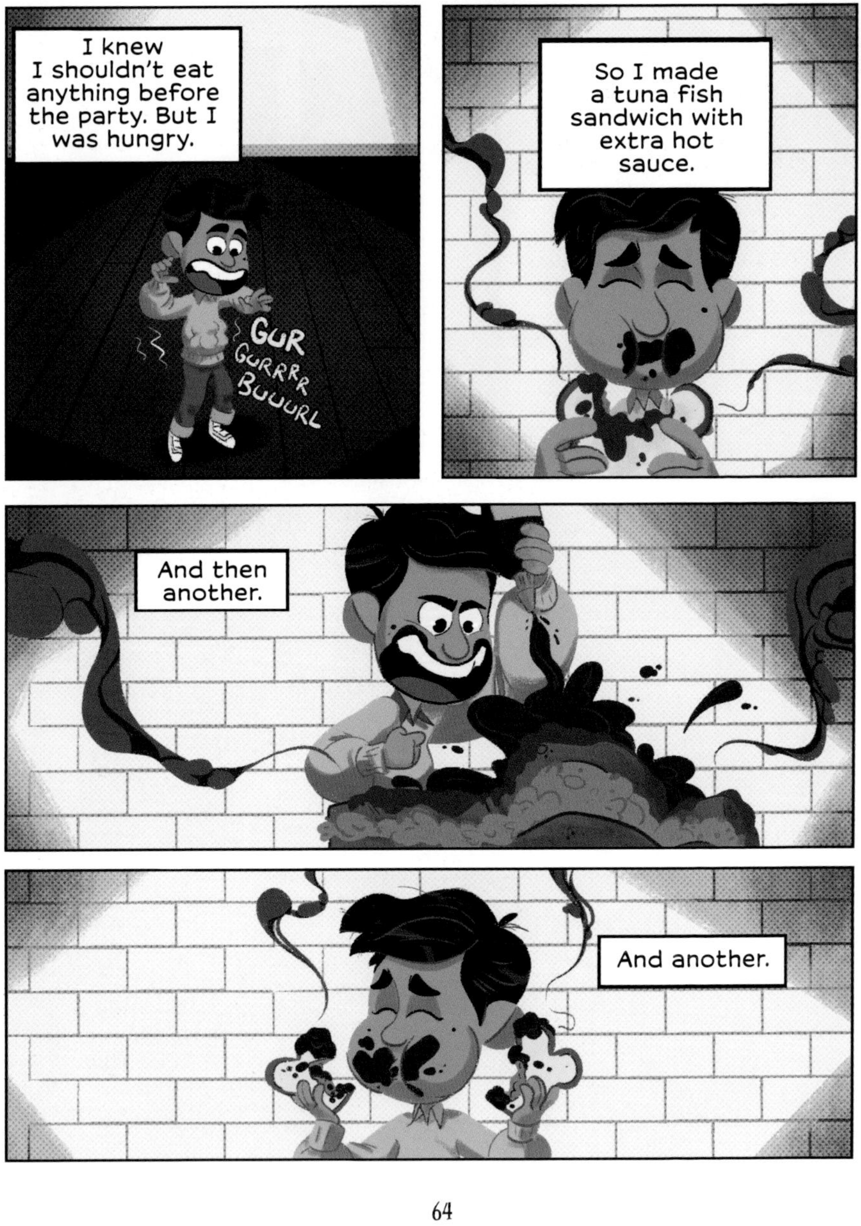
I knew I shouldn't eat anything before the party. But I was hungry.
GUR GURRRR BUUURL
So I made a tuna fish sandwich with extra hot sauce.
And then another.
And another.

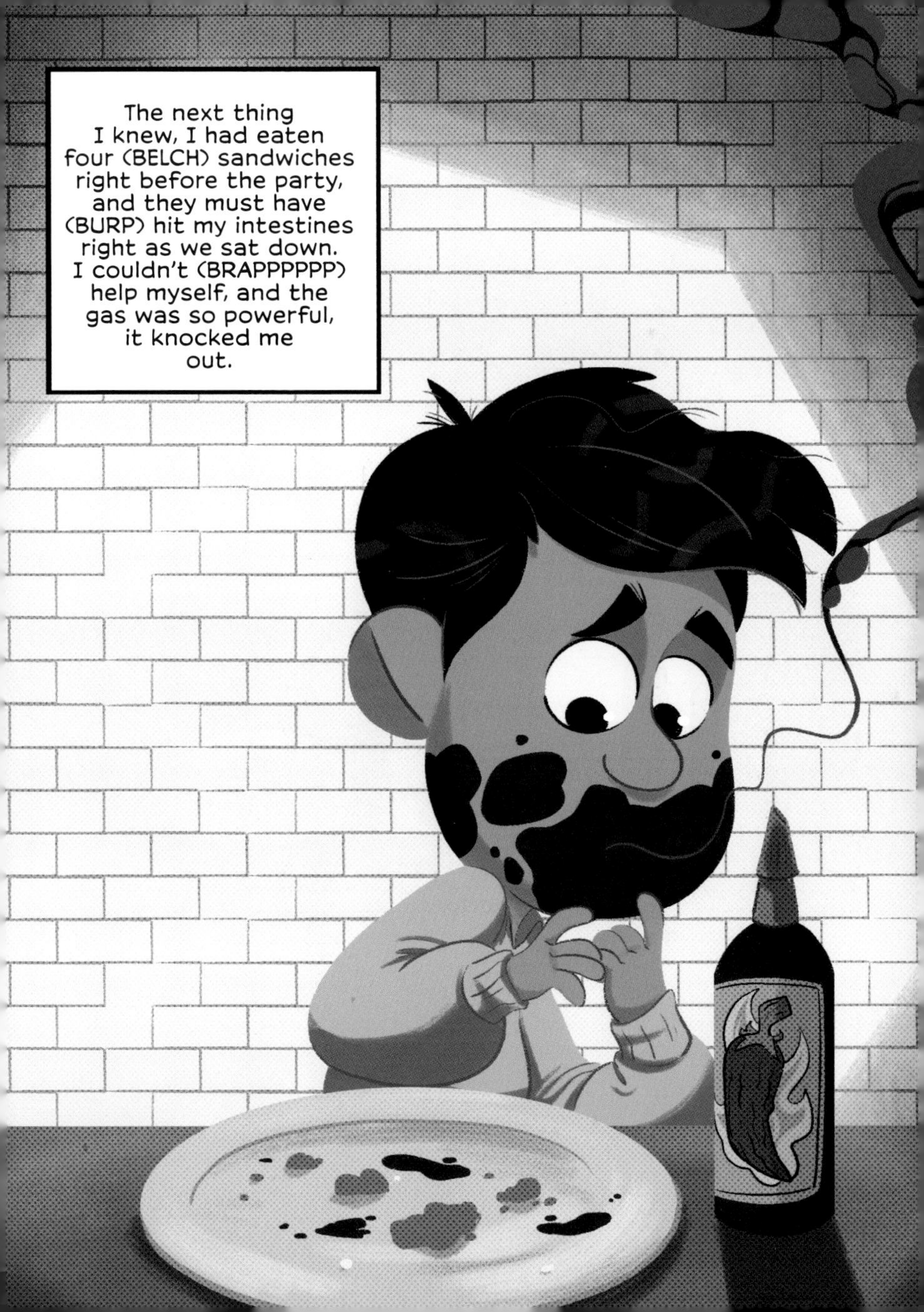
The next thing I knew, I had eaten four (BELCH) sandwiches right before the party, and they must have (BURP) hit my intestines right as we sat down. I couldn't (BRAPPPPPP) help myself, and the gas was so powerful, it knocked me out.

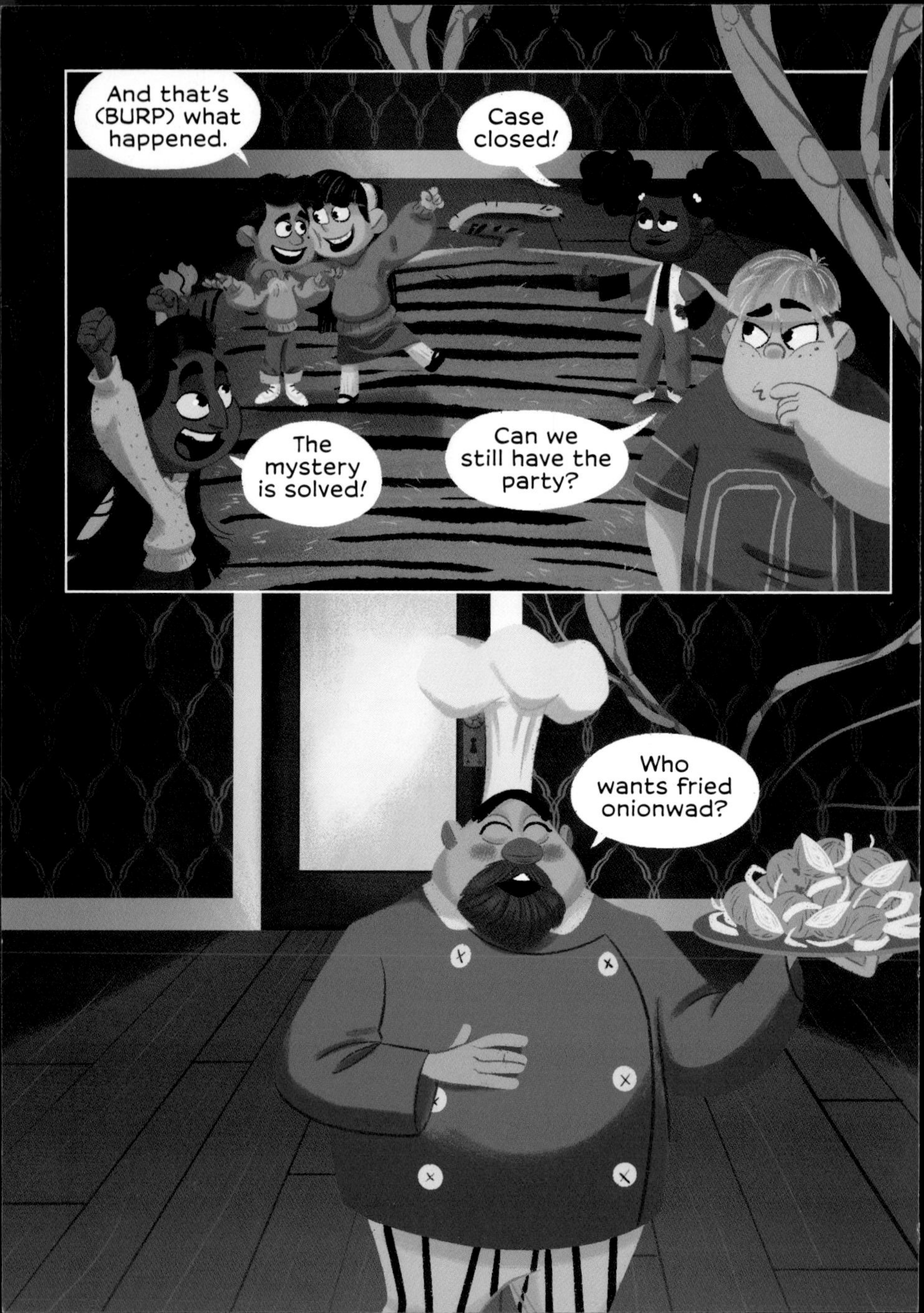
And that's (BURP) what happened.
Case closed!
The mystery is solved!
Can we still have the party?
Who wants fried onionwad?

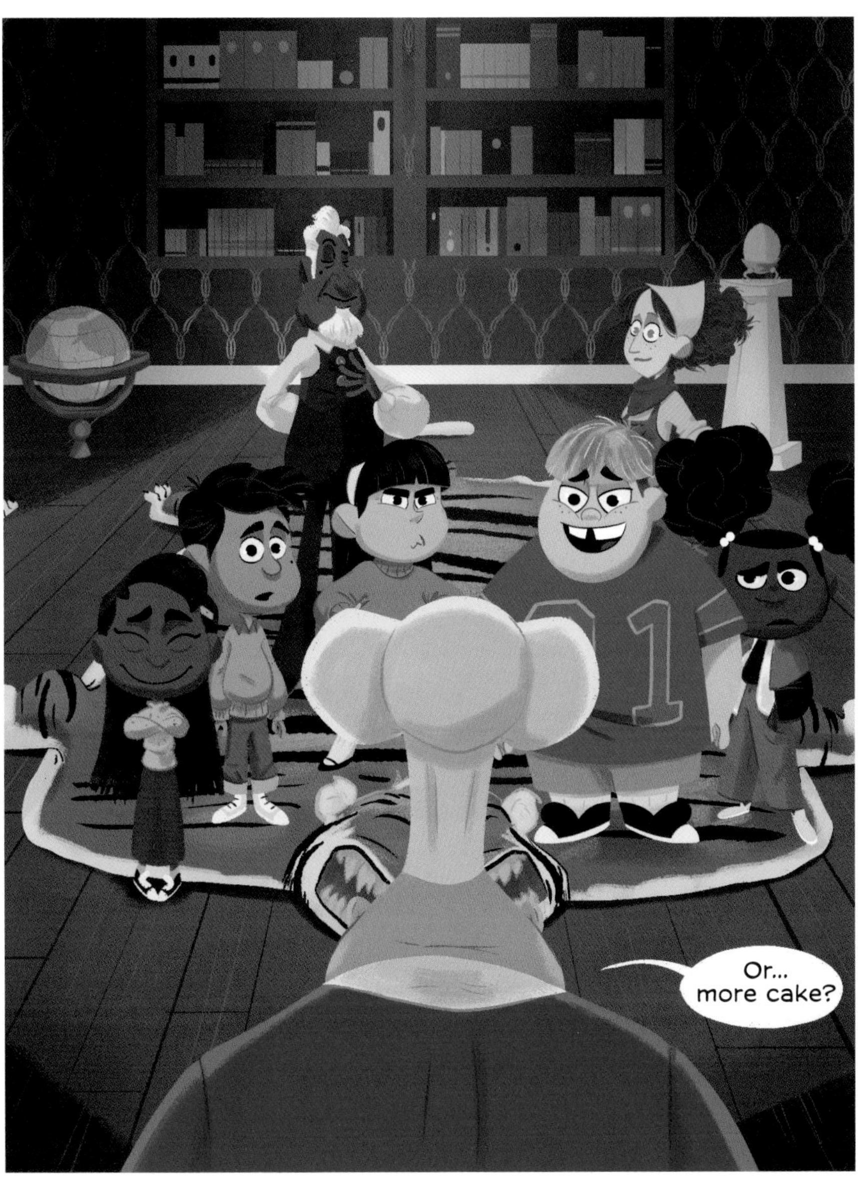
Or... more cake?

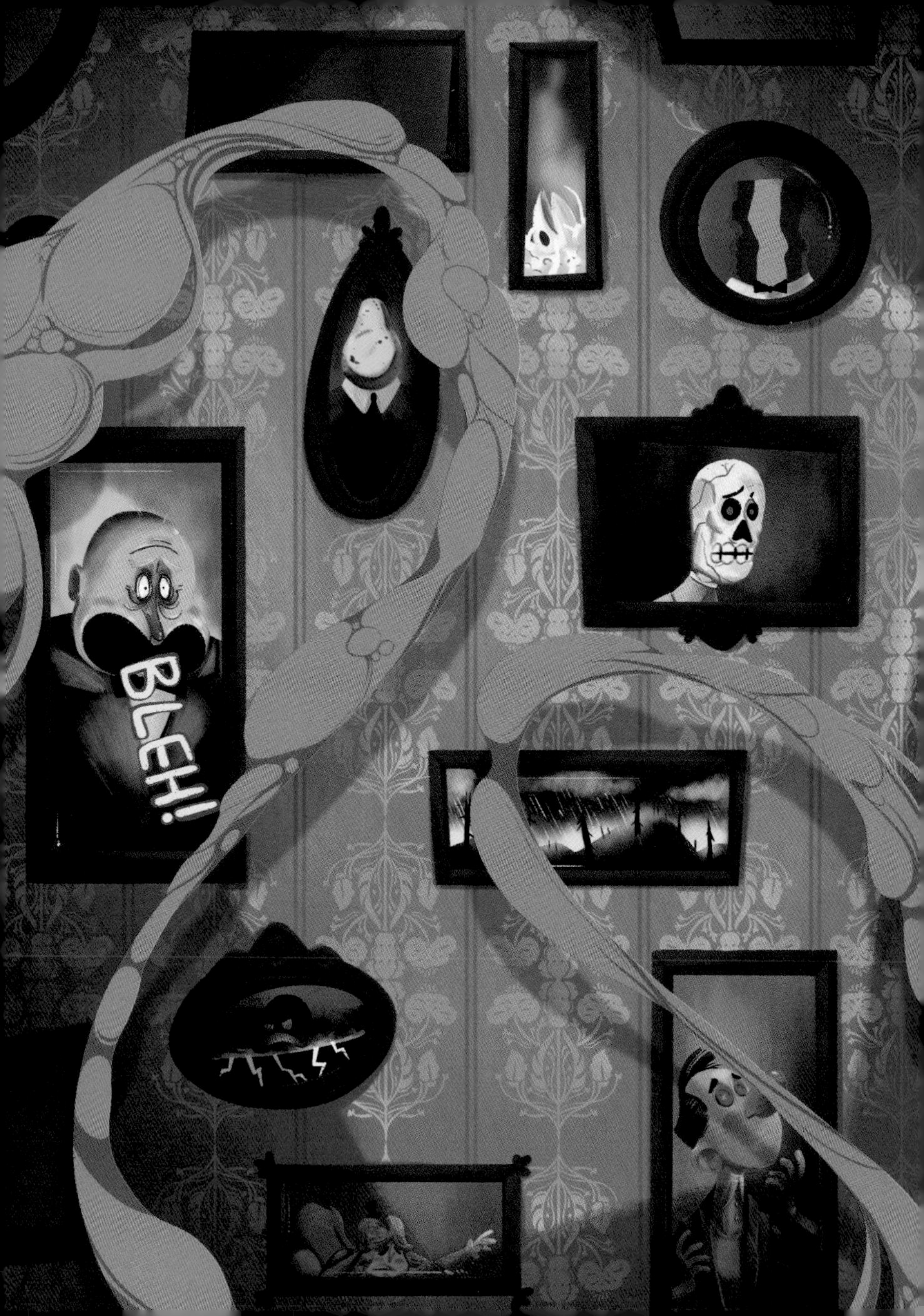
BLEH!

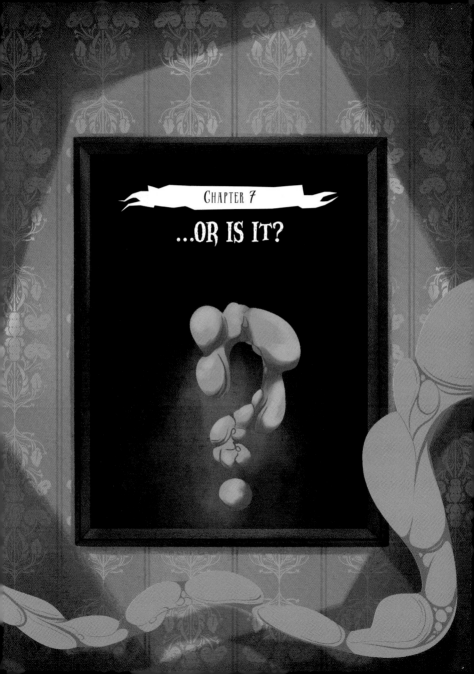

Chapter 7

...OR IS IT?

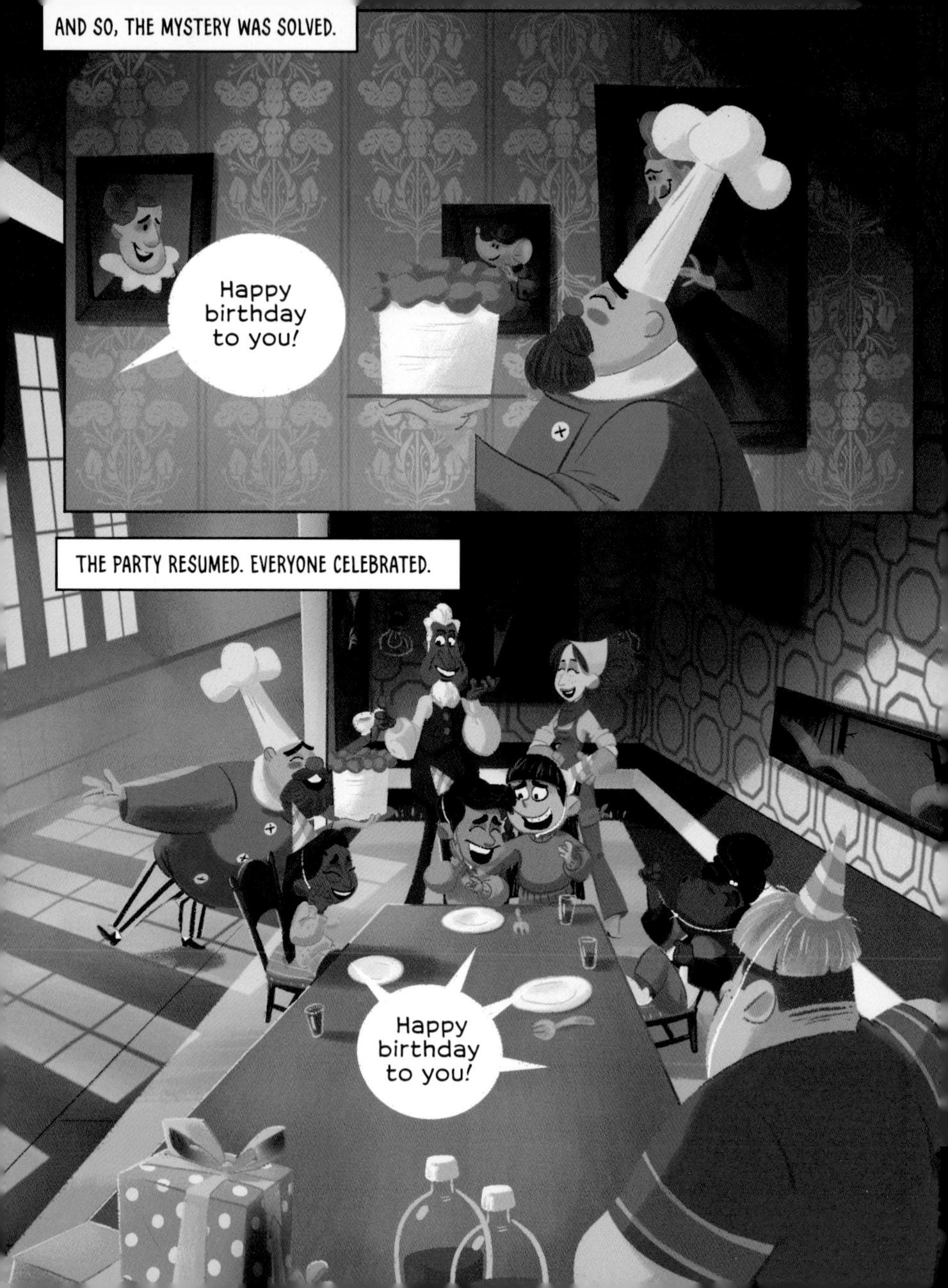
AND SO, THE MYSTERY WAS SOLVED.
Happy birthday to you!
THE PARTY RESUMED. EVERYONE CELEBRATED.
Happy birthday to you!

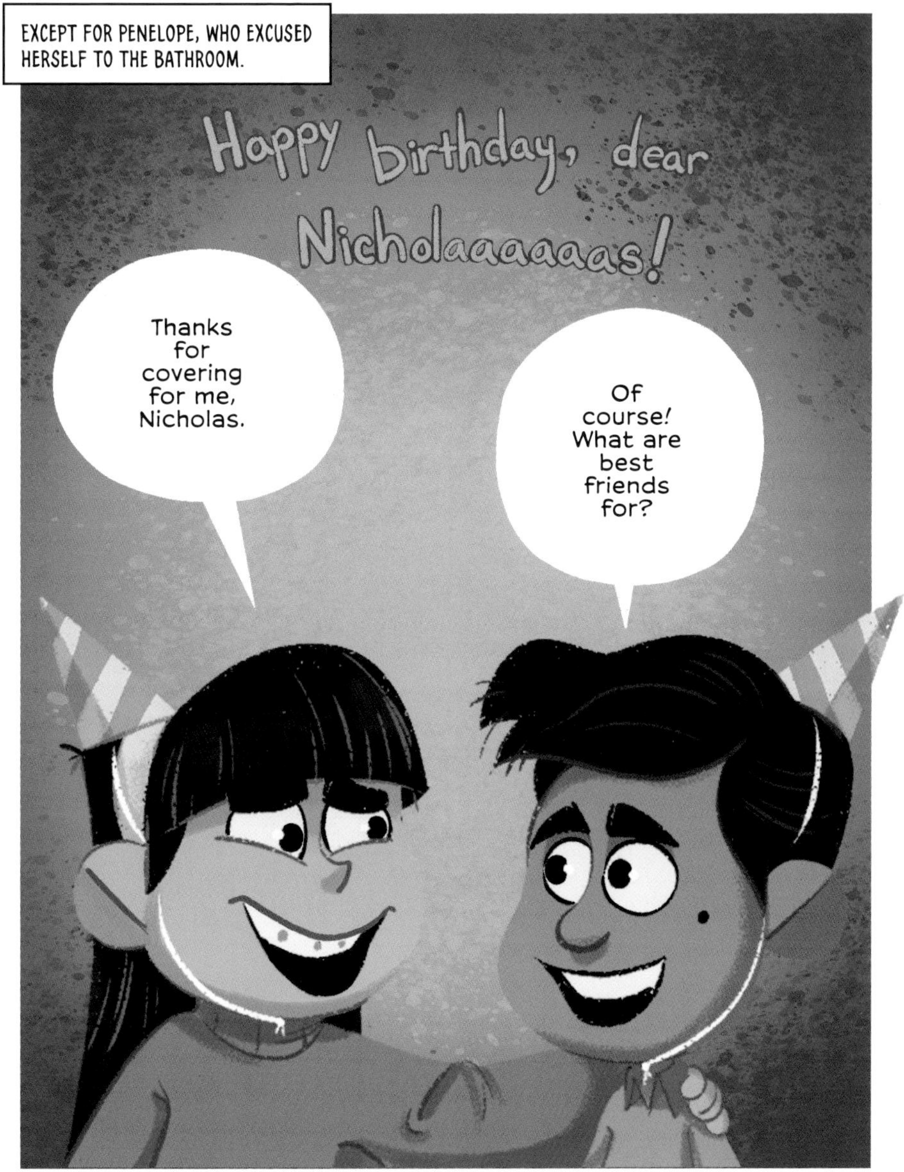
EXCEPT FOR PENELOPE, WHO EXCUSED HERSELF TO THE BATHROOM.
Happy birthday, dear Nicholaaaaaas!
Thanks for covering for me, Nicholas.
Of course! What are best friends for?

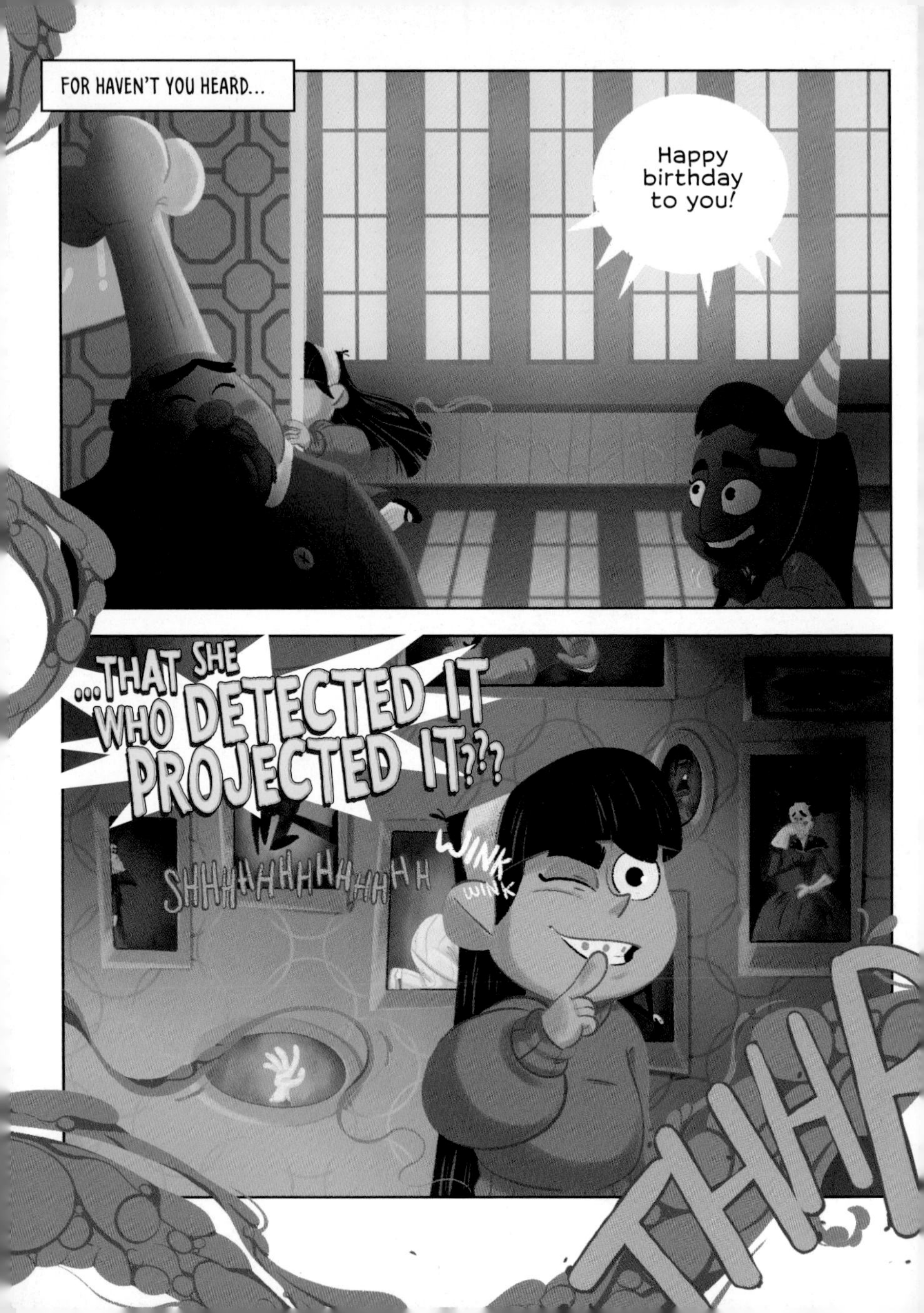

FOR HAVEN'T YOU HEARD...
Happy birthday to you!
...THAT SHE WHO DETECTED IT PROJECTED IT???
SHHHHHHHHHHHHHH
WINK WINK
THHH

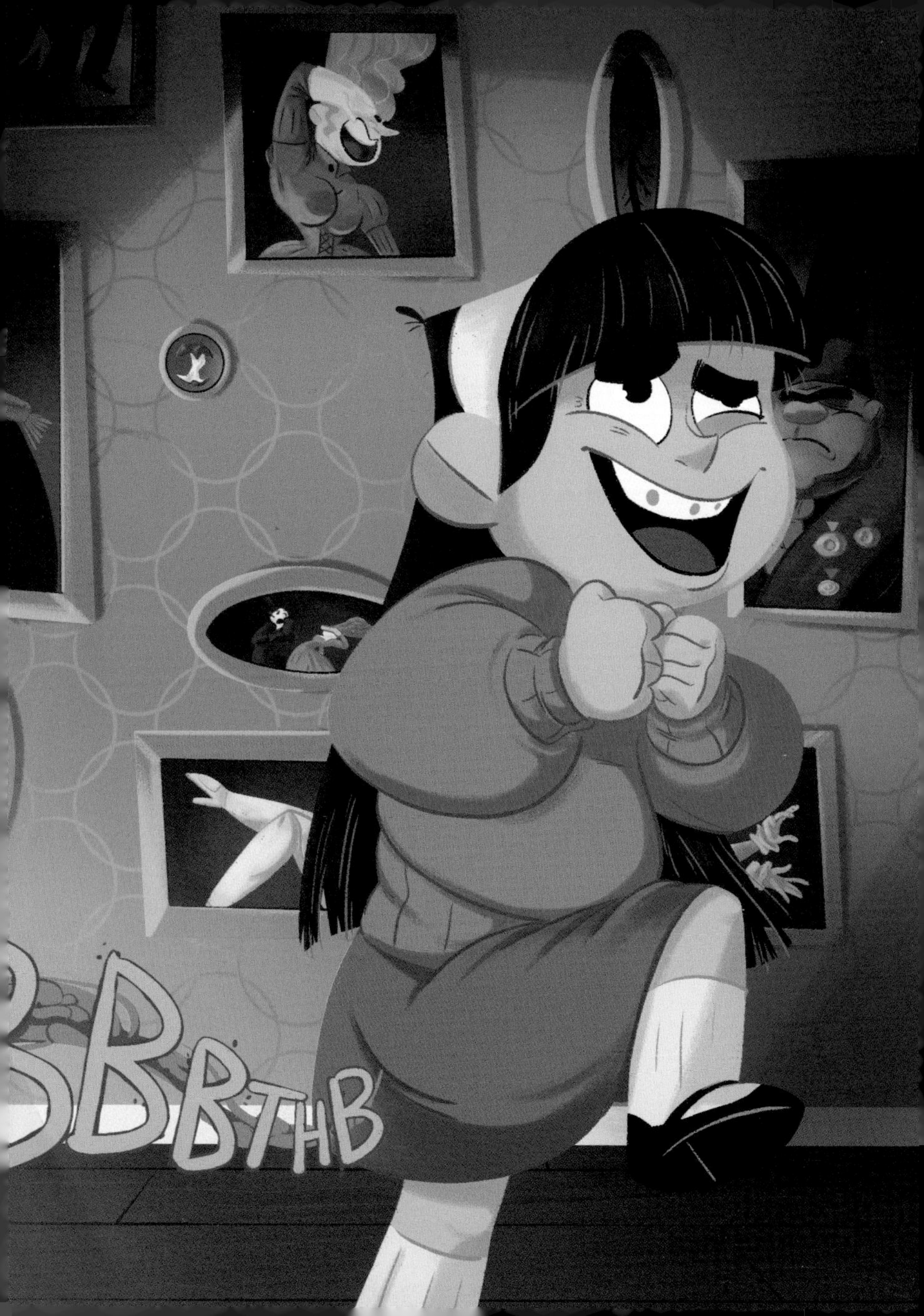
BBBTHB

You didn't laugh, did you? Good. Because solving mysteries is no laughing matter. I know it was unfair to have the detective be the culprit, but this business isn't fair. It is serious, though. Super serious. If you think you can stomach more mysteries like this one, I've got a file full of cases involving such untoward subjects as boogers, mustaches, and belly button lint.

Until next time.
S. Glum